The 1%

Copyright © 2015 by Bob Ford

ISBN-13: 978-1516811649
ISBN-10: 151681164X:

Published by Deerfield Park Press
New York, NY

The 1%

Bob Ford

Contents

Dedicated to
Every Wannabe

Married to Money

Like most things in Asher Brightendale's life, his attempted suicide was an example of high resolve, but poor execution. At just after nine p.m. Asher waded into the Long Island Sound wondering which they'd find first, his body or his Salvatore Ferragamo shoes which he'd placed on the beach next to his neatly folded Giorgio Armani sport coat. Finding the shoes first, he thought, would certainly add to the drama of his disappearance.

"He always overreacts."

"A clear play for sympathy."

"I expected penance, but this is a bit much, don't you think?"

Like a Greek chorus, the women's voices were as a clear and real in his mind as if the magpies of Centerport's gossips were standing right behind him. They seemed intent on extracting their pound of flesh and sending him to perdition bearing the last of their vitriolic derision.

"Do you know why you rejected me?" he shouted at his tormentors. "D'ya know why you hated what I did? I tell you why! Because you were afraid your husbands might do the same thing. And they would have, had they the chance!"

The tide at the western end of the Sound rises nearly eight feet. But at low tide - which was where it was at the moment - one has to go a considerable distance to find water deep enough to drown oneself with any degree of certainty. Given that Asher was not a strong swimmer, the prospect of his failing to reach deep water raised the specter of a botched job.

"That would be the final humiliation," Asher admitted to himself. "God knows what the guys would say at the club."

"Never been a closer."

"He choked."

"Talked a good game."

"When money was on the line, he could never sink the birdie putt."

He imagined the taunts came from a golfing foursome standing on the 18th green looking as if they had all just carded birdies. Asher wondered if everyone bent on suicide found themselves having to deal with phantom voices.

He shouted his retort at the empty beach. "You bastards are just jealous because I *got her* and you didn't!"

Asher was rapidly replacing resolve with indecision as he addressed the chorus. "For years you've all drunk my liquor and eaten my food and played on my tennis court. When you needed someone to get you into the country club or get your kids admitted into the Bountiful Country Day School or open doors on The Street, I was the go-to-guy - a Centerport man's best friend. Now you don't have the guts to look me in the eye. You know what that's a sign of? Guilt! Your lives are nothing but triple bogies. After I've killed myself, you'll be off the hook. I won't be around to remind you of that guilt."

The cold seawater was now wicking up his Brioni slacks and he could feel it trickle into his Polo underwear. How was he going to get into the deep water... really deep water? If only there were a boat. He looked back at the shore. No boats. Of course, there were no boats. Not on the Centerport beach. The realization only added to his growing animus and frustration. "So why in the hell would they call this Center*port*? How could this ever have been a port? Even our yacht club is in another town."

It is true of course, that in the traditional sense, Centerport is not the kind of port you would find in the dictionary under 'port.' But, in a more metaphorical sense, it is aptly named because there is a tacit understanding along the Connecticut coast that if you are "somebody" or if you are "anybody" aspiring to be "somebody," Centerport is where you live. It is from here that you can launch your social ship into the heady waters of Fischer's Island, Hobe Sound, and Lyford Cay or into the pages of Town and Country. So "Port" is not the misnomer that it would appear to be.

Even in his formative years, Asher understood the obvious advantages that an address in Centerport represented to his social aspirations. Isadora Partington represented his welcome mat. What she lacked in physical assets she more than made up for with the assets in her virtually inexhaustible trust fund. She had grown up with the knowledge that a limitless checkbook could prove to be more than an adequate compensation for God's oversights.

This is not to say that Isadora was unattractive, but she certainly never inspired appreciative glances from promising young men unless they had been made

3

aware of her wealth. Asher, who was counted among those who was privy to Isadora's pecuniary charm, was misled into believing the axiom that: *It's just as easy to fall in love with a rich girl as a poor one.*

He courted and married Isadora only to discover that the rest of the familiar postulate ends not in a period, but in a comma and goes on to say: *but it's a lot harder to live with a rich girl because she will never let you forget what her father did for you.*

For a short time, they lived in New York, but Isadora, whose view of the world had been constrained by the confines of Centerport along with a handful of fashionable and exclusive vacation retreats scattered randomly beyond the horizon, soon began to long for a return Centerport. Asher could not have been happier. Within a month they had taken an advance on Isadora's trust and purchased a substantial house on a modest hill - the elevation of which afforded a view of Long Island Sound from the maid's bedroom. While Asher found the physical house a befitting testament of the success he planned to achieve on Wall Street, he recognized that it lacked those exterior appurtenances which elevate one's home to estate category. In his haste to achieve social parity with the other properties on the street, he inadvertently alienated the McMurtrey's - his westerly neighbor - by cutting down the woods that served as a green barrier between their houses so that he could create a spectacular, half-acre, architect-designed, Japanese koi pond replete with fountains, waterfalls, decorative bridges and lily pads. Unfortunately, despite all of Asher's efforts and expense, the pond leaked and by mid-summer was little more than a mud flat peppered with dead koi fish.

Lavinia McMurtrey was not reluctant to share her rage with her circle of friends, "I've spent 29 years securely protected on the other side of the now missing forest. To say that I am aggrieved would be an understatement. Clearly Mr. Brightendale does not seem to understand that anyone in Centerport questing for social position would have done well not to offend me. Especially when one considers, as he apparently did not, that I command an important public following as author of the *Who's Doing What* column in the weekly Port Docker."

After an initial period of controlled hysteria, she penned a vitriolic column condemning Asher in an article entitled *The Wanton Destruction and Disregard for Centerport's Aesthetic Ambient Resources*.

"Lavinia," her editor pointed out, "your article on Asher Brightendale is libelous. Your neighbor, ill mannered and environmentally gross as he might be, was within his deeded rights to cut down any and every tree on his property and, if he wished, to seed the barren earth with asphalt."

She withdrew the article and instead initiated a word of mouth campaign that nearly cost the Brightendales an invitation from the Welcome Wagon Lady to join the Newcomers Club until, as Isadora confided to a friend, "I had to bail Asher out. Socially that is, by reminding our potential detractors, and there are many closet detractors in Centerport, that I was, and still am, a Partington. I simply asked that they bear in mind what my Daddy's money and his many charitable contributions mean to Centerport."

The wholesale disposition of the woods was bad enough, but Asher further inflamed neighborhood displeasure when, in the process of positioning his guest house and six car garage, he authorized the construction company to dynamite a substantial outcropping of fundamental Northeast granite bedrock. The reverberations broke several windows, caused the Darlington's Yorkshire to miscarry and shook down Beano and Sister Beaumore's collection of antique Lalique. Again, the wave of neighborhood protests arose, this time spilling onto the fairways and into the taproom of the Centerport Country Club.

While Asher was not one to ponder, in advance, the potential consequences of his actions, he did have a knack for damage control. The "explosion," as the Beaumores called it, necessitated that he summon his best efforts to mitigate the damage since the fallout promised to precipitate a serious setback to his quest for a prominent niche in the community. And so he did what had to be done in Centerport to turn public opinion: He showed them his money, or more accurately, Isadora's money. Asher began to aggressively court favor with Centerport's movers and shakers by hosting a series of lavish lawn parties replete with strolling waiters, live music and various entertainments. These included a troupe of white-faced mimes that performed magic tricks and who, reportedly, concluded their performance by making a good deal of Isadora's antique Sterling silverware disappear.

While the McMurtreys and Beaumores, along with those who courted their favor, refused to accept Asher's invitations, it can be said, that in the main, his campaign was adjudged a success.

Yes, money and its calculated display does have a way of helping one make new friends. But alas, Asher, egocentric and abrasively aggressive, was destined to find ways, even when not trying, to add to his growing list of detractors.

In fairness, however, it must be noted that some of Asher's public behavior was in fact a subconscious compensation for his marginal status in Isadora's eyes. Asher was never far from being reminded of the real source of his success.

"I know," she told her mother, "that he claims he's a success, but when I hear him bragging about how important he is, and he does it all the time in front of our friends, I have to step in and remind him that if it weren't for Daddy and his money he'd be nowhere."

In truth, a psychiatrist would probably have concluded that in Isadora's eyes, Asher had not succeeded in morphing himself into the image of her father.

For these and other reasons, not transparent to the community, their relationship grew more and more adversarial. Her apparent need to dominate, to humble and even, from time to time, to humiliate him in front of their friends became the source of much idle hour speculation. Which is to say it became a favorite item on the gossip agenda whenever two or more women gathered for lunch. Isadora took obvious pleasure in demonstrating that she held him on a tight rein and could upon short notice - or more often upon no notice at all - exact tangible exhibitions of his marital obsequiousness.

Despite a minor public tiff now and again, Asher's life was outwardly enviable and it appeared to those who peered up at the substantial house on the modest hill that this was a man who thoroughly enjoyed what life - and Isadora - had afforded him.

It was while sitting in the steam room at the New York Union Club that an old college friend said how much he envied Asher his happy life in Centerport.

"Happy life? Me? Wrong. I'm not happy. Do I look happy?"

"I thought you did," the friend said.

"Well it's a mask. A facade. I need a change. I long for a change. You don't understand what it's like to wake up day after day to find yourself confronted by that heavily mud brown creamed face on the adjacent pillow. And to see the engorged and growing love handles which are made for anything but love. I have to confess, for the last several years I have satisfied my needs with short lunchtime liaisons with...let's call them professional women. But that has been only marginally satisfying. More and more I find myself fantasizing about replacing Isadora with.... something... someone.... more of what I deserve in a wife."

"Do you have someone in mind?" the friend asked.

II

Enter Angeline Morris.

To say that she was beautiful would hardly do her justice. She was the "stuff" of fantasies. The cover of *Cosmopolitan* come alive. Long black hair, a full and perfect body and legs the likes of which hosiery manufacturers dream of for their ads. When she walked into a room men's heads snapped in a reflexive response followed by a furtive glance toward their wives to see if they had been successful in masking the truth of what had just transpired in their temporal lobes.

An objective observer would hardly have been surprised to learn that Angeline was afflicted with a near terminal case of narcissism. "I love the way I look. I love the way men look at my body. Even I can't get enough of me. I think of myself as the equivalent of a rare object d'art. Care must be taken. I eat an 80-calorie high fiber breakfast and then spend thirty minutes in a yoga exercise that I was assured will slow aging. Then I drive to the local *Fit and Firm* and spend two hours carefully and meticulously exercising each of my muscle groups. Toning…shaping…furiously attacking any erosion on the sculpted lines of my body."

Cellulite, of which she had none, was more ominous to her than death. She spent unconscionable amounts of money on creams and skin preparations and yet permitted her body to roast in the sun like some animal turning on a spit. She prided herself on the fact that her tan was always total. Her role in Centerport - and in Centerport every woman is supposed to have a role - appeared mainly to provide the benchmark by which husbands could tacitly measure the physical shortcomings of their wives.

On one occasion, Lavinia McMurtrey, intent on punishing Angeline for what she suspected her husband was thinking, attempted to inflict a modicum of punitive embarrassment by trapping Angeline into the tacit admission that she was both shallow and superficial. In front of a small and selected gathering of Centerport's more important women, Lavinia found an excuse to offer a litany of the positions she held in a variety of clubs and charities. "I support six charities, I'm on the board of three, I belong to three country clubs and am involved in virtually every civic organization in Centerport., And what, my dear, are you involved in?"

Angeline answered with a candor that defied response: "I'm involved in me."

It was clear that this was a woman who would not age gracefully. It was also clear, if only to Angeline, that the present state of her life needed serious upgrading. Her husband, who everyone called Boomer, had in her estimation simply not performed well financially. Not that he hadn't tried. But it seemed that the muse of Wall Street that had touched so many of Centerport's residents had deigned to pass him by. Angeline was unsympathetic.

"Boomer," she announced one night after dinner, "this is not the lifestyle to which I had planned to become accustomed. Our standard of living is just not up to Centerport standards."

"What are you talking about?" Boomer sprang to his defense. "We have a 7500 square foot home that is not exactly substandard housing. A swimming pool. A sailboat. I make $300,000 a year which, by most measures, is reasonably above the poverty level, even by Centerport's standards."

"But do we have a Maserati? Do we have a winter home in Lyford Cay? We don't even own a share in NetJets."

When Boomer's effort failed to stem the tide of Angeline's criticism, he simply refused to participate in any further conversations on the subject.

It was in early December that Isadora and Angeline happened to meet at the *Centerport Center for Reflexology and Centered Well-Being* and discovered their common interests.

"Oh, it's wonderful to find someone with a passion for holistic health and bottled water," Isadora said

"We should have dinner," Angeline suggested.

"Should we include our husbands?" Isadora asked.

"Of course. We definitely should."

"I'm sure we'll all become fast friends. Maybe we'll even travel together next summer," Isadora said as they left the *Center*.

Like most men before him, Asher reacted to Angeline with a lustful rush of intemperate ardor. Instantly he felt a primal need to impress her, to demonstrate that he was superior to the other men, that he not only deserved her unconditional admiration, but her body as well.

"I'm thinking about buying a Gulf Stream 5," Asher announced as he and Angeline chatted while Isadora entertained Boomer with her passion for things Holistic. "The old 3 just doesn't do it for me any more."

"You have your very own plane?" Angeline gushed.

"Of course. Flying commercial is such a drag."

Asher, who was never reluctant to expound on his accomplishments, was even more expansive than usual with Angeline. He peppered his conversation with detailed accounts of his exploits on the sporting fields at New Haven.

"Tail back. First string all four years."

Of his travels to the far reaches of the world.

"You really should see Bora Bora," he said casually.

Of his performance on the golf course.

"I have a 4 handicap."

And of success on Wall Street.

"We're up 38% this year."

Finally, he announced, "It is my intention to retire before I am forty and travel."

Angeline left Isadora's dinner party that night with a deeper appreciation for her sorry lot in life.

"Boomer," she said as they pulled out of the Brightendale's driveway, "let me just say that you either have to improve our financial position or I might just have to start looking elsewhere."

Boomer took her ultimatum with detached resignation. "I'm doing the best I can. I hope that it's good enough. But if you want to look elsewhere, be my guest." That she accepted his invitation would have surprised no one who really knew her.

The day after Isadora's dinner party, Asher left early for his Saturday round of golf. He played terribly. He simply could not concentrate. Her perfume, her eyes, the pleasure of looking at her body, it was all consuming. Short of the fact that she was without an independent source of income, she was everything that Isadora was not. He fantasized walking into restaurants with Angeline and watching men stop in mid-bite to gaze in awe at the creature on his arm. Here was a woman who would dazzle his business associates, give new dimension to his lawn parties. They would command center stage wherever they went. She would be the queen of his domain. Together they would become the golden couple of Centerport.

"Isadora, those people we had dinner with," Asher began two days later as if it were a passing thought, "Boomer and what's her name. Why don't you invite them to our next cocktail party? Let's have lots of people. Always more interesting if there's a crowd."

The reason he suggested a large gathering had nothing to do with his desire to assemble an interesting crowd, but rather the certainty that it would be easier for Angeline and him to remain inconspicuous at a party where the crowd is engaged in vapid conversations and are generally oblivious to anything but the whereabouts of the hor d'oeuvres.

The evening had barely begun when Asher managed to corner Angeline in his den. "Your perfume. Are you wearing Caron's Poivre?" he asked.

"At $2000 a bottle? Don't I wish," she replied.

"A woman like you deserves to wear no less. But then I wouldn't mind seeing you . . . in less," he smiled thinly.

"Why Mr. Brightendale...are you suggesting . . .?" her tone was laced with innuendo.

'Wishing," he said making no effort at subtlety.

They had not conversed for more than several minutes before her hand found reason to touch his arm, to make a gesture that gently brushed his neck. Quickly he lost the train of her conversation and had no idea if his responses displayed even a semblance of coherence. All Asher knew was that she was definitely interested in exploring this new emotional terrain. As his mind plotted how he would arrange their next encounter, he heard her say something about having been to the

Metropolitan Museum once and getting lost. There it was.

"You must," he said, "come into the City and let me show you *my* Metropolitan. We'll do lunch first at Masa,"

"That's the most expensive restaurant in New York," she said

"Really? Never noticed," Asher said casually.

Asher made the reservation for the following Tuesday. They had barely finished the chilled Almas Caviar when they both knew that an irrevocable course had been set. In each other they had found the answer to their separate needs.

"Next Wednesday? Lunch? Daniels?" Asher asked Angeline as he walked her to the Centerport bound train at Grand Central.

"What time?"

"Oneish?

"And afterward?" her smile added an unmistakable invitation.

Asher gave her a kiss on the cheek and whispered in her ear. "Let's see what comes up."

There followed that requisite period of clandestine meetings in which the main topic of discussion was where and when to meet again. This gradually gave way to the creation of questionable fictions delivered to their respective spouses to cover the increasing amount of time their relationship was requiring.

"I have a late client meeting," Asher explained to Isadora, "You know one of those god awful dinners with tedious people from the mid-west. And if it goes too late, as those bores seem never to want to quit, I might just stay in town."

When Boomer found his wife packing an overnight bag, Angeline, who had not expected him to work from home that day, quickly offered the first explanation she could think of, "Mildred Pierce was my dearest friend in college and she's being deported."

"Deported?"

"Or something like that. Maybe she said divorced. Anyway, she needs someone to comfort her and asked that I spend the night. I can't refuse."

By June, the time had come to launch their divorce strategies. Asher suggested that Angeline tell Boomer first to be sure that there were no complications. Angeline, showing a surprising, but definite tendency toward self-preservation said, "No, you first. I don't want to be hanging out on the limb if you get cold feet." Then, unintentionally giving voice to her paramount concern, she added, "And if Isadora takes you to the cleaners financially and you end up living in a garage somewhere, we may have to . . . " her voice trailed off and she changed the subject in hopes that Asher had not grasped the implication in her comment. She need not have worried. Her hand was on his thigh and his love-addled mind was impervious to anything but the suggestion that they find a hotel room.

III

Asher's approach to informing Isadora of his desire for a divorce was not exactly a textbook example of how a man should extricate himself from a marriage.

"Isadora, I've been thinking," he began. "Guilty thoughts actually."

"Guilty thoughts?"

"I have come to the realization that I have been a totally inadequate husband and that you deserve better," he said doing his best to sound sincere.

Isadora, sensing that possibly she had whittled down his self-esteem to a dangerously low level, responded by promising to become more loving, more understanding and suggesting, in a rare display of self-effacement, "No Asher, it is you, not me who deserves better."

"Actually, I think you're right." For Asher, there was no turning back. "I do deserve better. And for me, better is Angeline Morris. I want a divorce. We're in love. I am not ashamed to admit that we've had any number of liaisons in the City. We can't get enough of each other. After the divorce we plan to live here in Centerport."

"It's my fault," she cried to her mother. "This is all my fault. My constant carping ... constantly reminding him of the importance Daddy and my money have played in helping him get where he is on Wall Street. I accept full responsibility for driving him into another woman's arms. I will do penance for the rest of my life," she sobbed.

Isadora's penance lingered for about twelve hours before she decided that contrition did not become her. On the other hand, delivering punishment did. She took steps to have Asher and all his clothes removed from the house and piled them in the driveway. What followed fueled the Centerport gossips for weeks.

"Those are your clothes," she screamed as she poured kerosene on them and lit a match. "And this is me setting them on fire."

"Yeah.? Well this is your flower bed and this is me on the riding mower driving through your nasturtiums," he shouted back.

Having thus set the tone for the divorce proceedings, they retreated, Isadora to the substantial house on the modest hill and Asher to a single room in the adjoining town.

Asher put in a call to Angeline, "Ok, I've done my part, now it's your turn."

Where he had to bear the oral lashes of his wife's extensive vitriolic vocabulary, Angeline had to endure abject humiliation. She broke the news at breakfast, timing her announcement just minutes before Boomer would have to leave to make the 7:10 train.

"I want a divorce," she announced without explanation.

To her utter dismay, he took the news with serene detachment. In fact, it looked to her as if he was slightly relieved.

"Ok, if that's what you want, let's do it. By the way, we're out of orange juice." he said as he started for the front door.

Angeline befuddled by his passive acceptance, stood up and shouted at him. "You could at least have the decency to get angry. Or at the very least, you could have asked Why? Or Who?"

The wound inflicted by his apparent lack of ire left an emotional scar upon her psyche that was, in its way, second only to the discovery some five months later of the first signs of upper lip wrinkles. That night Boomer packed his bags and, with no more feeling than he would have shown were he reminding his wife to pick up his shirts, said, "Let me know when you get a lawyer so that we can get this thing settled."

Two weeks later, Asher and Angeline took up temporary residence in a rented apartment. At first, the unrestricted proximity and the opportunity to satisfy his appetites on a daily basis managed to obscure Angeline's more basic flaws. But as the newness of their concupiscence gave way to the realities of learning to live with one another, Asher slowly began to discover what Boomer had known for years: Angeline was truly in love only with Angeline.

Their first argument was precipitated when Asher, growing increasingly less tolerant of Angeline's affinity for mirrors said, "What is it with you and mirrors?" Asher tried to sound as if his question was no more than a gentle, humor-tinged prod. "I'm beginning to wonder if you intend to take up permanent residence at your make-up table."

What began as a small irritant grew steadily and was compounded by her inability to dress for an evening out without complaining that, even with three closets of clothes representing the better part of what had been Boomer's discretionary income, "I have absolutely nothing to wear."

In public, Asher found that instead of enjoying the envious stares of covetous men, he was more likely to find himself being questioned by security guards as to why he was loitering outside ladies' rooms.

"You want to move along bud? I seen you standing here for the past half hour."

The allure that had initially intoxicated him faded and as sobriety returned, Asher made a crushing discovery: "I don't understand it. I've been abandoned," he told his steam room college friend. "Nobody calls us. Nobody invites us to their parties. The women don't talk to Angeline and they won't even let their husbands talk to me."

The realization of his total rejection was indeed a traumatic blow to Asher. He had expected that once they had become an item, they would be assimilated into the fabric of Centerport society and thus assume their place as the community's most envied couple.

"My wife saw me talking to Asher at the bank and gave me hell," the tall golfer on the first tee said.

"Giving you tips on how to have an affair, was he?" laughed his partner.

"What did Asher expect?" said a heavy set woman at the Snooty Fox Nail Salon to the diminutive blond at the table next to her. "That we would abandon Isadora in her time of trial?"

What Asher did not understand was that Centerport is a matriarchal society. It is the women who, filling the daily vacuum left by their commuting husbands, make the decisions as to who is socially acceptable and who is not. Even the neophyte in Centerport quickly discovered that if two women should decide that they want to be friends, their husbands - even should they suffer an immediate and mutual aversion - had better learn to get along because they will see a great deal of one other. However, if the opposite were the case, the only time the two men would see each other would be on the golf course or on the commuter train.

Faced with a rapidly deteriorating affair and near total social ostracism, Asher let it be known he was having second thoughts." I'm thinking that maybe...well, that I just might considerer asking Isadora to take me back,"

Isadora, who was not looking forward to having her orderly life disordered by the lack of a compliant husband, agreed to let him come back so long as he was prepared to meet certain conditions. "No more trips to the City. You will cancel your account at Masa. You will find a job here in Connecticut. You will agree to whatever punishment I decide to hand out for as long as I decide to hand it out. I will likely decide to have you wear a GPS tracking device and if you should ever think of leaving, you'll leave with only the change in your pocket."

In short, were he to agree, Asher knew he would become little more than an electronically monitored indentured servant. He recognized that were he to accept Isadora's demands, his life would be difficult, at least for awhile, and he would have to appear in public with a look of sincere contrition to satisfy the Centerport women. At the same time, it occurred to him that he might preserve some of his ego by reminding the men that he alone had *known* Angeline.

Had he been more personally secure, he might have picked up his Gucci luggage, and whatever else he could have carried in his Testarosa, and departed for points west. But so great was his need for social acceptance in Centerport he agreed to Isadora's demands. However, instead of social acceptance, Asher endured a kind of tacit, but nonetheless odious, humiliation from his friends. He became a *How to Deal with Marital Infidelity* case study for the women of Centerport to emulate should their husbands decide to stray. It was at this low point that he had made up his mind to show them all and walk into the sea like James Mason at the end of *A Star Is Born*. But like most everything else in his life, he ultimately lacked resolve and after spending less than fifteen minutes up to his knees standing in the low tide of Long Island Sound he returned to the beach and sat down.

"Where the hell are my shoes? Who the hell took my shoes?" The final humiliation. Scavengers had descended on the beach and taken his shoes even before he'd drowned himself.

He returned home that night, barefoot. Isadora, who had gone to bed early, never inquired about the salt encrusted slacks she found in the kitchen the next morning.

In time, the women of Centerport grew bored of discussing his transgression and demonstrated their fickleness by returning to his parties, drinking his liquor and eating his food. To those who knew him only casually, he seemed to be the same old Asher. But to those few who knew him well, it was obvious that he had changed. He seemed, well . . . shorter. The old arrogance had gone begging. The aggressive confidence was held in check. He never mentioned Angeline. He did his duty as Isadora had decreed it.

Isadora, on the other hand, talked constantly about Asher's infidelity as though her survival of the affair had somehow elevated her to a higher level of human understanding. "I feel I have been through the fire of spousal infidelity and come out a stronger, more understanding woman."

She became a self-appointed counselor, a woman of experience who could be counted on to help others through similar travails. When she heard of a woman with marriage problems, she would seek her out and share the details of her ordeal with the wayward Asher and conclude with the admonition that all husbands are suspect.

And Angeline? Well, to quote from a letter written to a friend a year after it all ended: "I was the only one who ended up behind the short end of the stick."

Three months after she asked Boomer for a divorce, the Wall Street Muse touched down at his desk when a little Internet stock that he had purchased jumped 93 points in two weeks. He cashed out with a six million after tax profit. Boomer quit his job, let his hair grow and took up residence in the South of France. Sojourners from Centerport have reported seeing him on the beach at Antibes with scantily clad women.

Angeline left Centerport within the year and rented an apartment in Philadelphia where she worked, for a short time, as a runway model until she gained more weight than looked good in a size four. Eventually she married a man from Piscataway, New Jersey, who owned a car dealership and there she lives comfortably and belongs to the best country club. Lavinia McMurtrey bumped into her once in New York at a hair salon. "Well I would be less than truthful if I did not confess that Angeline is still striking, but on the other hand, it appears she is not aging gracefully."

A Minor Indiscretion

The first man Tolova lived with was a student at Julliard who aspired to write opera, worked nights playing piano in a neighborhood bar and sang Sundays with an oratorio group. Their single room was in a fifth floor walk-up in Greenwich Village. "Our lives are like Mimi and Rodolfo of La Bohème," Tolova told her friends. "We are poor but happy bohemians...well, sort of happy," she added tentatively.

Then one snowy evening life mimicked art and like the third act of La Bohème they stood in the snow outside a subway station near Washington Square and Tolova bid her oratorio singer *Addio Sansor Rancor*.

"Goodbye and no regrets," she said as she headed down the subway steps.

Her second lover, Gabin, was a French artist who lived among his spent paint tubes and canvases in a large unheated loft in Montmartre near the Sacre Coeur. He often recited poetry as he painted Tolova in the nude against the snowy Parisian backdrop outside their window.

> "Roses za are red,
> Violet za be blue
> Your body ees hot
> I love painting you."

"Je gèle mon cul!" she barked as the winter wind found its way unabated into their room raising a second set of goose bumps on her body.

Translation: I'm freezing my ass off.

Gabin laughed, "Fortunately, I am not painting zat part of your anatomy."

The year Tolova turned twenty-seven she caught pneumonia and decided she'd had her fill of the arts and would look for a lover whose career pursuits were less artistic and more fiscal in nature.

"I've decided to find someone," she wrote to a friend, "who can keep me warm. Preferably in a Sable coat."

The transformation from her *Bohemian Period* to her *Pragmatic Period*, was both dramatic and total. She returned to New York and within less than a month began an affair with an insurance executive named Percy Bagwell who was married and living in Scarsdale.

"Me? You're giving this to me? A Credit Card? My very own credit card? What a sweetheart," she cooed to as she secured the card in her purse.

The insurance executive responded in a voice full or prurient intent, "I expect to see frequent charges from Victoria Secret."

It wasn't long before she discovered that the credit card not only worked at Victoria's Secret, but at Oscar De La Renta, Giorgio Armini, Chanel and Tiffanys.

Bagwell's American Express bill jumped out at him like an IRS audit notice, "$85,000!" As he scanned the list of charges he blanched, choked and began to sweat, all the while doing his best not to say anything that would dampen the anticipated pleasure of their noontime coitus.

"I'm sorry, sweetie," she said doing her best to sound loving and contrite, "I really, really do my best to look for sales."

"Sugar pie," Bagwell responded, "this is a little more than I planned for you to spend. I think maybe it's time we give the card a little rest."

Tolova's incensed response was not at all what he expected. "Maybe it's time I give you a little rest," she spat back. "And speaking of time, don't you think it's time for you to divorce your wife?"

Good grief! Divorce my wife? What does this little tart think this is all about?

The insurance executive from Scarsdale counted himself truly fortunate when Tolova announced she was giving him back his credit card and checking out of his life. "Any man," she said in parting, "who would be dumb enough to give a credit card to the woman with whom he's having an affair, is not smart enough to be having an affair."

With the residual of the affair having left her elegantly clothed and heavily bejeweled, Tolova was ready to step into what she called her *Acquisition Period.*

"No more lovers. This time a husband." Her criteria were basic. The man had to be rich. Uber rich. Age was not a factor in her search. In fact, advanced age - i.e. one foot in the grave - she considered a plus. She required that the target had to be able to move about without a walker and had not as yet found it necessary to rely on frequent changes of Depends.

"With a body, a face and a brain like mine," she told herself, " I am convinced I can hook a really big fish."

Her fishing expedition generated five potential candidates. Of the four on her list who took the bait, Toddinger Meriwether Brubecker, or Dinger as he was known to intimates, was adjudged best qualified to provide her with the lifestyle to which she wished to become accustomed.

"I am proud to say, Tolova," he began while downing his third martini at La Cote Basque, "my perspicacity, my cunning, my intuitive understanding of the financial world has netted me a fortune of nearly 450 million dollars. Plus or minus a few million or so. But who counts?"

"Not me," she answered demurely.

An initial impediment to their budding relationship was that Dinger possessed a wife of forty-six years who traveled incessantly in pursuit of her passion for things other than Mr. Brubecker. It was on a Tuesday that Dinger provided Tolova with the news she'd been waiting to hear. "I have, shall we say, remedied the inconvenience of my marriage with what I regard as a generous settlement which will permit my ex-wife to pursue her passion for archeology in the Yemen desert."

No sooner had the justice of the peace blessed their nuptial than Dinger made it clear he had no intention of letting himself be drawn into anything that even remotely resembled his former domesticated life in the suburbs. Tolova offered her assurance that she fully concurred with his vision of their life together. "Children? Out of the question. A dog? Never. A maid? We don't need one. A place in the county with all those mosquitoes? No thank you."

Poor Dinger. He brought none of his business acuity to his relationship with Tolova. This tower of Wall Street intellect never fully understood how within four years they had two children, a dog, a maid, a cook and were living in Centerport, Connecticut.

II

"Dinger dear, look at this," Tolova said handing him a formal looking letter. "Our house has been picked to be in the Decorator Magazine's Showcase issue. We'll be in print."

When Dinger agreed to build them a house, Tolova insisted she be her own architect and then orchestrated the interior decoration after having summarily dismissed Mario Buatta. The result was hailed in the decorator magazine as a monument to eclectic bad taste. The reviewer wrote:

> "In the middle of what presumably
> was intended to be an open atrium,
> I came upon a fountain featuring a
> large naked nymph holding a fish.
> It was intended, I believe, that the
> water was to flow through the mouth
> of the fish into the circular pool.
> However, for reasons apparently
> relating to a fault in the plumbing,
> on the day of my visit, all the water
> appeared to be passing through her
> private parts. I suggest they name the
> fountain: *La dame pipi dans la piscine.*"

One must concede that what the Brubecker's lacked in taste, they made up for with their money. Generous donations in the right places do tend to induce a form of retrograde amnesia in towns like Centerport.

I love this town because the name of the game here is money, Tolova thought as she parked her Maserati next to a fire plug on the town's main street. *If you've got money it means control. And when you have control you have power. I have them all.*

Tolova learned to play the control game among the uber rich and even the filthy rich with virtuoso aplomb. Her money - or rather Dinger's money - earned her entree to the best county club, the most coveted community organizations and a seat on the boards of every prestigious charity. Once inside, she worked diligently to infiltrate the membership committees thus giving her the power to accept or reject whom she pleased. She dropped black balls like hail stones.

Tolova's attitude was that those with power should never hesitate to use it, even in the most mundane of circumstances.

For example, her five-year-old son played in the town T-Ball league. When he told his mother he had been benched part way though the game, she immediately went to the phone.

"Coach Tuber." Tolova made no effort to temper her annoyance. "I demand to know why my son was taken out of the game in the fifth inning. He is clearly the best player you have."

"Mrs. Brubecker," Coach Tuber said, "there are fifteen boys on the team and only nine are permitted to play at any given time. I have to give everybody a chance. It's only fair."

"May I remind you," she retorted, "as the T-Ball coach your role is not to be the dispenser of *fair*, but to win games."

Tuber was taken aback, "Win games? We don't even keep score. I'm sorry Mrs. Brubecker, but if you don't approve of the way I coach, I suggest you either take your son off the team or apply for the coaching job yourself."

Instant umbrage. Tolova immediately promoted Coach Tuber to the top of her retribution list. Some three years later, when the coach's name appeared on the list of proposed new members at the country club, she took her measure of revenge and dropped a black ball. "Coach Tuber is just not our kind of people," she told the membership committee.

Dinger was mostly oblivious to his wife's penchant for inflicting social punishment on those she found deserving. But he was well aware that Tolova seemed determined to dress in a provocative manner guaranteed to display her figure so as to engender the appreciative glances and approbations of other men.

"You're not going to the club dance looking like that, are you?"

"Of course. I love this dress. You don't like it?"

"You're exposed on top and you look like someone poured you into the bottom."

"I hate to admit it," Dinger told his sister who harbored a deep distrust of Tolova, "but I have begun to suspect that Tolova might be looking to have an affair."

His sister's concurrence served only to heighten Dinger's anxiety which, in turn, fed into a deep well of latent suspicion.

Tolova, if the truth be told, was tempted to have an affair as she did not regard Dinger as Mr. Excitement when it came to their sex lives. It was during one of Dinger's critical assessments of her attire that she responded with two telling questions, "Can I help it if men find me and the way I dress attractive? Am I to just ignore them?"

"I put up with her suggestive behavior at first," he confided again to his sister, "but I've gotten tired of her incessant flirting. So, in a manner of speaking, I'm yanking her chain, reeling her in, confiscating her checkbook and making her disappear from Centerport for a while."

Tolova was distraught and made no effort to hide her distress. "Dinger, I can't believe you'd do such a thing to me."

Endure her penance she did, though the fact she served her exile at the Golden Door Spa softened the punishment considerably. Such was her predilection for the restoration of access to his checkbook, she emerged from her imposed isolation contrite, ready to dress modestly and behave per her husband's dictates.

It wasn't long after she returned to Centerport that Dinger decided to atone for what he had begun to regard as an intemperate display of spousal abuse. "Tolova, I have decided that I've been much too hard on you. To make amends, I've rented a 200-foot yacht - with chef and crew - to sail the Greek Isles. I think it would be nice if you were to invite two other couples to cruise with us."

"Like who? Maybe Isadora and Asher Brightendale?" she offered eagerly.

"No, I don't care for that over-libidoed Asher and we both know she gets sea sick. How about Pooh Armbruster, Bunny Stablemoore and their husbands?"

Oh, God! Tolova thought to herself. *Two more disgusting men do not exist on this planet.* She was especially put off by Yogi Armbruster who got his nickname because he had a face like Yogi Berra and a body like Yogi the Bear.

Tolova smiled appreciatively at Dinger doing her best to hide what she was thinking; *I know what he's is doing. He chose men who are flirtation proof. He wants to be sure I won't be tempted. Tempted? To do what? With him lurking?* Realizing that Dinger was not about to consider backing off his choice of cruising partners, she feigned enthusiasm, "Dinger dear, I think they would make wonderful traveling companions. I'll invite them right away."

To understand what, on the cruise, was to become the seminal event in Tolova's life, one would first have to appreciate the immensity of Yogi Armbruster's derriere. To put it plainly, gravity seemed to have conspired to pull down much of his substantial girth to his behind. In truth, he exemplified the pejorative term *fat ass.*

It was after a particularly excellent dinner, complete with unconscionable amounts of red wine, that the indiscretion occurred. Deciding they needed a healthy dose of night air to mitigate the effects of the wine, Yogi, Yogi's wife Pooh and Tolova started to climb up a narrow ladder that was normally restricted for use only by the crew when accessing the upper deck. Unfortunately, Yogi got stuck in the hatch at the top of the ladder which was too narrow for his ample posterior. Finding herself staring up at Yogi's prodigious behind, Tolova, having succumbed to the judgmentally dampening effects of red wine, turned to Pooh and said, "Maybe if I goose him it will pry him loose. Should I?"

For years afterward there remained considerable speculation as to whether Pooh actually granted Tolova permission to goose her husband or if Tolova simply misinterpreted what she took as Pooh's nod of approval.

Unfortunately, at the very moment Tolova reached up in an attempt to dislodge Yogi's derriere via a firm goose, he managed to squirm free and turn his body to start back down the ladder. Tolova's goose missed its mark and became a full fledged frontal assault. Yogi yelped in surprise followed by Tolova's immediate apology.

"Ooops! Sorry 'bout that," she said choking back an embarrassed laugh.

Tolova hoped that her apology would be enough for Yogi to dismiss her minor indiscretion as a playful goose gone-astray.

As she backed down the ladder she found herself thinking, *The last thing I want is for Dinger to hear about this. I know he'll take it the wrong way. Even with Yogi.* Later that night Yogi informed Pooh that what looked like a goose was not a goose at all.

Pooh was aghast, "She grabbed your penis and all she had to say was 'sorry about that?'"

Next morning, Pooh, acting as though the assault on her husband's private parts had been a personal affront, cornered Bunny Stablemoore on the poop deck and, after eliciting a pledge of utmost secrecy, shared the details of what she described as Tolova's purposeful molestation of Yogi's genitals.

"I must tell you," Pooh confided, "I will never to speak to that wanton woman again." Realizing where she was, Pooh qualified her intent, "After we get off this boat, of course."

Once back in Centerport, it became readily apparent that Pooh was doing her best to distance herself from Tolova. It was during a chance meeting with Bunny at the Snooty Fox Nail Salon that Tolova sought to learn the truth. "I don't understand it, ever since we got back from our cruise Pooh has been avoiding me. She hasn't even called to thank me for the trip. Every time she sees me at the Fit and Fitness she hides in the bathroom. Do you have any idea why she's acting like that?"

Of course, Bunny knew why. *But I'm not about to elect myself the messenger. Tolova shoots messengers. Since what she did to Yogi is none of my business, I am going to tell a little white lie.*

"I have no idea why Pooh is avoiding you," she said at last.

"Well, I've waited long enough," Tolova said. "I've got to find out."

Tolova called Pooh and was immediately rebuffed. "Why would I want to talk with a woman who had the audacity to grab my husband's penis? If you were looking to have an affair..."

Tolova cut her off sharply, "Looking to having an affair? With Yogi? Believe me, Pooh, if I'm going to have an affair it's not going to be with some 300-pound man whose ass is so big it gets stuck in a boat hatch." It occurred to Tolova that she needed to know if Pooh had been so indelicate as to talk about her minor indiscretion with anyone else. "Does anyone but you know about ... about...what happen on the boat?"

"Well, I told Bunny and Isadora Brightendale. And I will have you know that I was shocked...shocked to learn from someone I will not name that you have goosed Isadora's husband as well."

Tolova could not believe her ears. "Who told you I goosed Isadora's husband?"

"I can not reveal a confidence," Pooh said.

" I never! I've never touched Asher Brightendale," Tolova denied vehemently. Then it hit her. "Wait a minute did you say you told Bunny?"

"The next day...right after it happened," Pooh said.

Her shock morphed into immediate anger. "Bunny knew? Bunny knew? Why didn't she tell me? I asked her to tell me why you were avoiding me and she said she didn't know. She lied to me."

Despite Tolova's resolve to avoid doing anything that might give Dinger pause, he remained on the lookout for signs that Tolova might be unfaithful. His vigilance led him to surreptitiously listen in on Tolova's phone conversations. After she hung up on Pooh, Dinger approached her with what he'd heard.

"You have no right to listen to my phone conversations," she shouted.

"I have every right to know if it's true that you goosed Asher Brightendale?"

"Of course it's not true!" she was near tears.

"Then why would Pooh Armbruster say Isadora claims you did? To goose Yogi was bad enough. But Asher? Knowing him, he'd take that as invitation."

Within minutes, a frantic Tolova with an angry, fuming Dinger in tow, were sitting in Asher and Isadora Brightendale's living room.

"Asher," she said frantically, "tell Dinger that I've never goosed you. Tell him that's it's not true," she pleaded.

Asher, who was yet to have his affair with Angeline Morris, was fully aware that his wife suspected him of being less that totally faithful when it came to Tolova and was impatiently waiting for his answer. He realized that the Brubecker marriage, and maybe his own, depended on his answer. "Dinger," he said, his voice full of assurance, "she's right. I've never been goosed by your wife. *On the other hand,* he could have added, but did not, *I have copped a feel of Tolova's behind last time I dance with her at the club. And I think she liked it.*

Isadora then added, "Every time I hear Pooh tell someone what happened between you and Yogi, she embellishes the story. No one knows what to believe."

"I'll tell you what you to believe," she said barely under control, "You can believe it was a totally innocent accident. Let me tell you what really happened."

Tolova's explanation sounded like Rosemary Woods explaining how she accidentally erased 18 minutes of Nixon's Watergate tapes. "And when he managed to unstick himself from the hatch, he started to fall back toward me. To keep him from crushing me I simply put up my hand . . .and....and ....

"And what?" Asher laughed, "used it as a handle?"

35

His attempt at injecting humor only drew a cold and silent rebuke from his wife.

It is not certain what Dinger finally believed. Had Pooh given Tolova permission to give Yogi a friendly goose to help unstick him from the hatch? Had his wife accidentally or purposely fondled Yogi's private parts as he was about to fall on her? Was there any truth to what Pooh said about Tolova goosing Asher? Answers were required and Tolova supplied one.

"This is all Bunny Stablemoore's fault."

"Why is it Bunny's fault?" Isadora asked.

"Because she knew why Pooh was avoiding me and she lied about it. If she'd told me the truth, I could have prevented Pooh from spreading her malicious and wild distortion of what actually took place on the boat."

III

.

When word leaked out in Centerport about Tolova's misdirected goose, her many detractors labeled her with the sobriquet *Phantom Gooser*. Coach Tuber saw in the leak his opportunity to avenge Tolova's black ball. He sent her a goose with a note that said: *A goose for Centerport's most famous gooser. This goose is cooked and now so is yours.*

Meanwhile Yogi, who had originally only suffered a slight indignity and minor assault on his privy parts, found himself the butt of the salacious quips that permeated the links at Centerport' Country Club.

"You know what they're saying about Tolova grabbing Yogi's penis?" a bald golfer on the third tee asked.

"That it was no big thing," roared the skinny man who has just chipped out of a sand trap onto the green.

When the foursomes' laugher died down, a short fat golfer asked," When you putt for a par and miss the hole it's called a bogie. What do you call it when you aim a goose and miss the hole?"

"A Yogi," the other three golfer's chimed together.

Unable to put an end to his current public perception as the punch line to a joke, Yogi announced that he and Pooh had always longed to live in Idaho.

When Dinger informed Tolova of their departure, she looked upon their exodus as self-inflicted chastisement and a tacit admission that they had falsely accused her of Yogi's molestation. Now she was left with only one more score to settle. She let it be known that Bunny had done her a grave injustice which was simply too egregious for her to reveal. She would only be placated with Bunny's social exile.

"She's punishing me for not telling her the truth," Bunny confided to Isadora Brightendale. If I had told her, how would that have made any difference? And to tell people that I was guilty of some grave injustice. What? For not having told her that Pooh was mad at her because her goose of Yogi went wide of the mark?"

Isadora encouraged Bunny to fight back when she discovered Tolova had managed to have her name dropped from invitations to all those affairs that matter to Centerport society. But Bunny, forbearing and non-confrontational as she was, could not conceive of mounting a counter offensive that would provide more fodder for the town gossips. She hoped Tolova would, in time, simply turn her attention to more deserving social miscreants.

"Who do you side with, Tolova or Bunny? I mean you have to choose," the president of the Centerport Beau Artes Society asked the ladies who had just concluded their discussion of the literary merits of *Fifty Shades of Gray.*

"That's easy," answered a blond woman with mild acne. "How many parties does Bunny throw each year? How many social events does she control? One, two?"

"Poor Bunny," the president said, "I must admit, I'll miss her, because I do like her better than Tolova."

Bunny suffered her social ostracism in dignified silence until one Centerport hostess made the mistake of inviting both Tolova and Bunny to the same sit down dinner party for twenty-four. The hostess compounded her faux pas by placing Tolova immediately across the table from Bunny.

When Dinger arrived at the party and realized that Bunny was among the invited guests, he pulled Tolova aside and warned, "I want you to behave yourself tonight. Just ignore Bunny. I don't care what awful thing she did to you. Pretend she's not here. Let's avoid any kind of scene."

Tolova did not appreciate the admonition." Dinger, how can you think I would create a scene with that snake? I will say nothing and be the most docile of guests."

But four glasses of wine washed away any resolve Tolova might have had to restrain herself. It was during an innocuous discussion on the sorry state of Centerport education that she erupted. Bunny, who up to that point had said little, offered "I must say that I am very disappointed in what appears to be the inability of the teachers at the Bountiful Country Day School to teach even the basics of good composition."

Tolova had suppressed her desire to put Bunny in her place long enough. "I don't see where you get off making critical statements like that, after what you did to me."

Secretly and fervently everyone at the table had been hoping for a confrontation. Maybe the ignominy that Bunny was said to have perpetrated would surface at last.

Tolova continued, "Knowing, as you must have known, that I would be on the guest list tonight, I can't believe you had the gall to accept our hostess's invitation."

Everyone fully expected that Bunny and her husband would say nothing and simply excuse themselves and beat a hasty exit. They did not.

Inappropriate a venue as the dinner party might be, Bunny decided to defend herself. "Tolova, I guess this is as good a time as any to explain in front of our friends the reason I did not tell you why Pooh Armbruster was avoiding you. It was because I felt she was over reacting to what occurred on the yacht. I assumed that she would eventually decide to let the incident pass and forget about it. All you'd done was attempt to goose her husband and it certainly wasn't your fault that at the last minute he'd turned and you grabbed his manhood."

"Tolova did what?" the hostess exclaimed to her dinner partner.

"Grabbed his penis," the man to her left whispered an explanation.

"Were they having an affair?" the hostess asked in a hushed tone.

"With fat Yogi?" the man to her left responded with a laugh.

Bunny's so called grave injustice had finally come out. Tolova turned red. She attempted to speak, but the words became a log jam in her throat.

Bunny was not done. She stared directly at Tolova. "I never believed Pooh's claim that you purposely grabbed Yogi's penis and I wanted to spare you and Dinger the embarrassment of what, at the very most, was only a minor indiscretion resulting from too much wine. As to people in Centerport calling you a phantom gooser behind your back, well, I'm really sorry about that."

Bunny sounded as if she almost meant it. Slowly the titter that had begun next to the host at the far end of the table evolved into laugher that began to make its way from one guest to the next suppressed only by those who were concerned about Tolova's penchant for retribution.

A waiter appeared at the door and announced, "Coffee and aperitifs will be served in the living room."

The catering service waiter's interruption served to give everyone an excuse to begin escaping the scene. Dinger was up first and spoke to the hostess. "Thank you," he said lamely. "We need to go. I've an early day tomorrow."

He took Tolova by the arm and pulled her in a less than gingerly manner toward the front door. Accounts of Bunny's performance quickly made the rounds of Centerport's gossips. Dinger decided to absent himself from Centerport and traveled to Africa to hunt big game. Tolova stayed at home, adopting a much lower community profile. In time the discussion of the incident ran its course and was mostly forgotten by all but those who, over the years, had been subjected to Tolova's social wrath. Dinger unfortunately, contracted a rare parasite while shooting in Kenya and Tolova buried him a year later. Once Dinger was in the ground and his checkbook in her hand, she enrolled her son in prep school and began the post-Dinger phase of her life.

"I would like to have you route me to Cap Ferrat," she told the travel agent, "but with a stopover in Paris for a day or two." The reason for the visit was that since Dinger's demise she had found herself thinking about her years in Montmartre. *I wonder if by any chance Gabin might still be painting in his loft? I could afford to keep him now.*

Scene change. Paris. Montmartre. The limo Tolova had hired pulled into the square near the Sacre Coeur. The small building housing the loft was still there, but it appeared to have been vacant for several years.

"Driver, you've got to find a way in?"

"No problem," the driver said as he checked the entrance. "Ma oui, the door she is wide open."

As she walked up the stairs and into what had been their single room and Gabin's studio, Tolova realized that he had probably continued to live there for a number of years after she left and that, in all likelihood, had been its last resident. As she rummaged through the clutter he'd left behind, she came upon a half dozen partially finished canvases.

"Nudes. Nothing but nudes," she said to herself. "All signed by Gabin." For a brief moment she expected, or at least hoped, she might find one of her. None were. She picked up the last of the nudes and held it under the skylight to see it better. The woman was seated in front of their loft window. The trees outside were winter bare.

"She looks cold." Tolova said aloud. "She's got to be freezing her ass off. Je gèle mon cul!"

And then from somewhere though the years she thought she heard Gabin's voice, "Fortunately, I am not painting zat part of your anatomy."

She stared at the painting for a long moment and then, as if the woman in the picture might answer, Tolova asked, "Did you catch pneumonia too."

The Prodigal Daughter

"Puff, puff, puff, wheeezz, puff."

Cosima Kinsley's body folded, unfolded, and then pivoted first to one side and then the other as though she were an unwilling hostage trying to free herself from the Velcro straps that secured her to the Butt Buster. It was a complex and formidable-looking contraption that in former times might have passed for a torture device.

"Puff, puff. Shit! Puff, puff" She worked the intricate series of pulleys and counterweights, busting a butt upon which there really wasn't all that much to bust. "Oh, I hate this." She leaned back and stared at the ceiling. "This is utter torture!"

"So why do you do it?" her husband asked as he began to search the refrigerator for something to serve as breakfast.

"Oh, Christ, Fletch. Have you looked at the lard on my ass lately?"

"There isn't any."

"Says you."

This "I'm too fat" "You're *not* fat," discussion, if one could call it that, took place at least three times a week. Cosima was definitely not the person that the guy in the T-shirt and shorts was yelling at through the TV. She didn't need a Butt Buster, or Thigh Thinner, or Hips Helper, or Tummy Tucker, or any of the other anatomical annihilators that UPS periodically dropped at their door.

"Cosima, if you had any less fat on your behind, you'd cut right through the upholstery every time you sat down. You're not fat!"

"And you're not funny, Fletch." She rolled her eyes, signifying that it was futile to argue with him."Puff, puff, puff, wheeezz, puff."

The first time Fletcher Kinsley saw Cosima, he was twenty-three-years old, on his hands and knees, scooping wet coffee grounds into a paper cup with a plastic spoon. It was only his second day as a salesman at Jack Poor Motors in Centerport, Connecticut. He had accidentally knocked over the coffee pot in the break room, spilling the soggy grounds and sending shards of Pyrex into every corner. Unable to find a broom and dustpan, he had resorted to the cup and a plastic spoon. He felt ridiculous and hoped to have the mess cleaned up before anyone discovered him. He happened to glance up, and there she was, staring at him.

Cosima was dressed in what he later came to call her I'm-marching-in-a-protest clothes. She wore a long sack-like, recycled cotton dress with a braided rope wrapped around her waist. On her feet were large platform, walking sandals, secured with wide Naugahyde straps. To show her symbiotic relation with nature, she had woven flowering herbs in her hair, giving her the look of a garden gone to seed. Fletcher noticed that she wore no make-up and let her hair fall naturally where it might, encumbered though it was with all the herbs. Her natural state seemed only to validate her innate beauty. He could not help but notice how her ample, firm breasts refused to be denied acknowledgment as they pressed against her Mother Hubbard attire. In her limpid blue eyes, he sensed the hint of a latent sexuality lying in wait like a hungry jungle animal ready to spring on its prey.

Years afterward, she would tell people, usually in front of Fletcher, that she had stopped in to her father's car dealership to use the bathroom during a protest march against the unethical treatment of whatever was on her protest menu that week. In retrospect she could not explain what it was about Fletcher that had stirred her passion as she looked at him on his hands and knees, spooning coffee grounds into the paper cup. "Something snapped," was the way she put it. He was an empty vessel needing to be filled. A paint-by-the numbers canvas looking for someone to apply the color. She began their relationship with a lie, "I'm looking to buy a car. Can you help me?"

Fletcher, having yet to make a sale for Jack Poor Motors, brightened immediately and stood up extending his hand to the wondrously unkempt, but very attractive, woman with the herb garden sprouting from her head. "Please excuse the mess, I'm a little new at this." He gestured feebly at the coffee maker. "My name is Fletcher Kinsley. Welcome to Jack Poor Motors. What did you have in mind?"

"A test drive," she said intently, her eyes searching his for some sign of mutual chemistry. "It doesn't matter what car; I just want a test drive."

The test drive didn't last long. They parked in front of his rented room in Eastport, the town where people who could not afford Centerport lived, and spent the next two days mostly in his bed where she drained him of his essential fluids.

Fletcher was well aware that no salesman at Jack Poor Motors was permitted to demo a customer for more than fifteen minutes. Two days was certainly over the limit. He knew that meant the end of his career as a car salesman. But he was so totally consumed by his passion for this insatiable woman, he didn't care. He had been dazzled, overwhelmed by the female whirling dervish that claimed his every waking hour. No woman had ever been so enamored of him. It was uncharted territory. To be wanted, to be desired, to be treated as a virtual sex machine was truly a heady experience. He was like a man on a concupiscent binge, lost in a delirium of euphoria that clouded his vision and impaired his judgment.

On the afternoon of the second day, as he lay on his bed, his physical resources depleted, his energies drained, too weak to register much concern over the loss of his job, Cosima revealed who and what she was.

Cosima, her real name was Cosimasuela Margacious Isabella after two grandmothers and an aunt, was not just the daughter of a car dealer, but the scion of one of Centerport's richest and oldest families, on her mother's side. That was *who* she was. *What* she was, was in a state of rebellion. She had decided to reject and renounce all that her mother and her patriarch grandfather, Ambrose "Bumper" McCoy, represented. Fletcher learned that, while her family's political sympathies were on the right, Cosima rode an outrigger on the left. Their pursuits were material; hers were philosophic. They cut down trees, she hugged them. They ate animals and wore their skins; she ate veggies and gave money to PETA. They wanted the homeless locked up; she marched in support of giving them voting rights.

Her protests were often for causes, or in

opposition to causes, that her parents had not even heard of. Cosima carried banners against wearing fur and joined the revolt against higher ATM fees. She protested the creation of casinos on reservations and then marched in favor of Indian rights. She protested against foreign oil imports, offshore drilling, fracking and then rallied for more and cheaper home heating oil and lower gas prices. When Fletcher pointed out that some of her protests tended to be in direct opposition to one another, she tossed his observation aside with a simple, "Nothing's perfect."

While Fletcher never joined her marches, on occasion he would drive her to a staging area. Often she would have to ask someone what they were protesting against. The only difficult moment in their courtship came when Fletcher wondered aloud if maybe it wasn't the *cause* that mattered to Cosima, as much as the pure joy of protesting–*anything.*

In retrospect, Fletcher realized that he should have performed due diligence on the woman with the head full of herbs. Had he managed to look at her more objectively and less lasciviously, he would never have married her. Unfortunately, as a man caught in the riptide of unrelenting passion, he was simply not capable of such detached analysis. She was the flame and he the moth. There was no avoiding her allure and every night, sometimes in the afternoon as well, he would seek her out to satisfy his growing addiction to the sweet ambrosia he found in her arms.

When not in bed, and when Cosima was not involved in a protest, he would call for her at home. The first time, knowing that he would meet her mother, he had worn a suit and arrived with flowers in hand.

Cosima deposited him in the living room, then abandoned him for a moment to run upstairs. No sooner had she disappeared than Mrs. Petula Poor entered the room. She was a large, imposing woman just under six feet tall who carried herself in an imperious way and made no secret of that fact that her wealth put her safely in the .01%. She had a manner of addressing lesser mortals with her head tilted back, while viewing them down the bridge of her nose. Her eyes took a quick inventory of the figure standing in front of her. She looked as if she had just discovered a stranger in her living room holding a bouquet of poison ivy and tracking mud on her oriental rug. Her first words were not "Hello" or "You must be Fletcher" or "It's nice to meet you," but rather, "Who are your people?"

"My people?" he repeated, not comprehending her question.

His apparent inability to fathom the nature of her question irritated her. "Your people. Where are you from? What does your father do?"

"Do?" he asked.

Exasperated, she shot back, "What I am asking, young man, is whether you have anyone who you might offer as a personal reference?"

"Well," he said tentatively, "I work for your husband."

"You work for my husband?" She was incredulous. "I wouldn't let that get out, if I were you. At least not in Centerport."

That was the highpoint of their conversation. Petula's interrogation took only a few minutes, but time enough for Fletcher to develop a large degree of sympathy for Jack Poor who, until that moment, he had found to be anything but a sympathetic employer. When Cosima finally rescued him, he was holding the flowers upside down behind his back. Cosima must have overheard much of their conversation, because she immediately took Fletcher by the arm, looked at her mother, and said simply, "You better get used to him. This is the man I intend to marry."

From that moment on, his fate was sealed.

II

Cosima's phone cell rang and she undid herself from the Butt Buster and picked it up. It was her mother. "Mummmmmy," she began. Her tone was obsequious and subservient. "I was just about to call you. Any sign of the colitis this morning?"

As Fletcher studied the face behind the phone, he found remnants of the woman he married, the one with the herb garden in her hair. Of course, her hair was different now. Very different. The lovely brown cascades that had fallen around his face as she rode up and down on him during those months of premarital sex in his one-room apartment had, somehow, been transmuted into long, blonde, frizzy strands that burst from her head in a million different directions. It seemed to Fletcher that no comb or brush would dare attempt to bring discipline to that mane.

"Oh, Mummy," her voice dripped with solicitous concern, "You must call Dr. Weiderman this morning and have him give you something. I just can't bear to think of you being uncomfortable the entire weekend.

She hadn't always spoken with her mother in such endearing tones. In fact, for years they did little but yell at each other. Her mother hadn't even shown up for their wedding, saying she could not bear to witness her daughter repeating the same mistake she had made by marrying so far beneath her station. In her place, Petula sent a lawyer with documents, officially revoking Cosima's trusts, canceling her checking accounts, credit cards, and generally casting her out of the family.

"I feel badly that your mother didn't come," Fletcher had said after the wedding ceremony, thinking that Cosima needed to be consoled.

"Fletch ... I don't care that she wasn't here. Look at me. You're looking at someone who is actually happy she didn't come. I have rejected her. And in rejecting her, I have been liberated from her money and her right-wing regressive politics. She doesn't own me anymore. You have no idea how I've hated being the rich Poor girl, having to put up with all those prep-school Ivy League types buzzing into our driveway in their Mercedes and Porsches, thinking they could corrupt me with their credit cards and country clubs."

"I kind of envy them," Fletcher said. "I mean, I'm driving a six-year-old Dodge Dart, and I don't belong to a country club, and I'm probably never going to be able to afford to live in a town like Centerport. Not a very exciting prospect for someone like you."

"Fletch, Fletch ... don't you understand? I married you because I want to live like *real* people in a *real* house, or *real* apartment, or even a *real* trailer park with *real* people. Not these Centerport snobs. I want to live in a real city like Detroit."

Detroit?

Detroit would not have been Fletcher's first choice or any numbered choice for that matter. And it probably would never have been on Cosima's list either. But fate had a hand in their decision. As they traveled west after their wedding, his 1990 Dart broke down on the Edsel Ford Parkway. Cosima immediately proclaimed their breakdown was a divine harbinger. She decided she had been called to serve in the urban desolation that was downtown Detroit. "Real people live in these hovels," she said. "People whose needs and causes I will make my own."

Fletcher acceded to her heady sense of purpose and agreed to settle in Detroit where he found a job with a car company. However, after a week in a rented room at the corner of Grand and River Road listening to gunshots in the streets, coping with aggressive drug dealers, and fending off drunks intent on grabbing a quick feel of her breasts, Cosima had an epiphany. She announced to Fletcher that the *real* people she was talking about actually lived just west of the city limits in the town of Livonia. And so they moved immediately and Fletcher became a commuter.

In Livonia, Cosima resumed her pursuit of activist causes. Unfortunately, with so many protest opportunities, she found it hard to focus on or stay interested in any one issue or cause for more than a month or so. While she was always asked to march or join a sit-in, it was evident to Fletcher that her dedication to any cause, including their marriage, tended to be transitory. What once he regarded as the curiously erotic affectation of a dilettante activist had, for him, run head long into the reality of getting on with their lives as husband and wife.

He did his best to ignore, and when that was impossible, to accept Cosima's determination to spend her days searching for ways to save Greater Detroit. Her mission, as she put it, was "to rescue the city from the social inequities perpetuated by a corrupt government and the residues of corporate pillaging." What he could neither ignore, nor accept, was Cosima's roller-coaster mood swings. She could ignite at the slightest provocation. It might be something as simple as him forgetting an item on her shopping list or as major as not getting an expected raise. Fletcher soon gave up trying to anticipate when, or even why, the next eruption would occur.

Living, as he did, in a state of constant uncertainty drained him of affection. This is not to say there weren't good times in their marriage, times when he'd fallen back in love with her. But there were more times when he was out-of-love. The imbalance slowly dimmed the distant vestiges of his original love for Cosima, leaving only small residues of feeling surrounded by an empty indifference.

Fletcher came to understand that time, and nearly fifteen years of proximity, had succeeded in transforming him, in her mind, into just one of the several appurtenances necessary to maintaining the appearance of family. But that was not all that had been transformed in Cosima's mind. The travails of the downtrodden had slowly taken a backseat to causes closer to home. When, six years ago, Wayne County, which is where Detroit is located, announced they were going to bus their youngest of two daughters, among numerous others, to a school in downtown Detroit to help relieve racial imbalance, she said, "Whoa!" meaning: Not with my daughter, you don't! She rallied like-minded mothers in Livonia to stage a protest. It was in vain. The decision to bus was irrevocable. At that point in her life, Cosima finally admitted to Fletcher that she needed money. Lots of money. A whole lot more than Fletcher was making. While his promotion to section manager at the car company provided a semblance of job security, it had little impact on his salary. Money became her obsession. With money, she was sure she could spare their daughter from the ignominy of becoming one of the pawns in remedying racial imbalance and send her off to private school. Her political pendulum was in full swing, and she announced to Fletcher that it had come time to end fifteen years of filial enmity and seek a rapprochement with her mother.

Fletcher drove her to the airport and bid her goodbye as she began her pilgrimage back to Centerport–a penitent seeking absolution. "I still say we don't need your mother's money. I can find a way to pay for private school." Cosima's response was a short, mildly derisive, "Ha!" She spent a week in her old home, showing proper remorse for the excesses of her youth. When she returned, she came bearing Petula's promise of regular and contributions to her checkbook.

In addition, Petula made immediate arrangements for their oldest daughter, Julie, to transfer to Miss Porter's School for Girls in Avon Connecticut and to spend her vacations in the cultured environment of Centerport. Their youngest, Hildy, was enrolled in The Bloomfield Hills Country Day School, just North of Detroit. At Christmas that year, Petula surprised her daughter with a Russian Sable coat. Cosima resolved to wear it only in her basement or when visiting Centerport out of deference to her two PETA-devoted

Livonia neighbors.

Fletcher came to regard Petula's beneficence as her way of belittling his less-than-stellar performance as a wage earner. Admittedly, the fount of money that had flowed into Cosima's checkbook improved their lifestyle. But at the same time it had, in subtle ways, diminished his status, even his importance, in the eyes of his children. They no longer had to listen to him say, "I'm sorry honey, we just can't afford it." Whenever his children needed money, they went directly to their mother, who denied them nothing. With financial floodgates open there was no way Julie and Hildy could know that their girlish joy and excitement at *being rich* fed and sustained his belief that he had failed his family. Fletcher suffered his humiliation in silence.

III

"Why are you looking at me?" Cosima hung up the phone and began to strap herself into the Butt Buster again. "You know when Mummy calls I have to talk with her."

"I'm looking at you because there's no one else in the kitchen to look at."

"No, no," she said, shaking at accusing finger at him to indicate she rejected his explanation. "I *know* that look of yours. Whatever you're thinking, I want you to stop thinking it right now."

"I was just thinking that I liked your hair when it was normal. Meaning *normal*."

Cosima let out an exasperated sigh. "Paulo-Marcel," Petula's hairdresser, who was always on stand-by when Cosima returned to Centerport, "loves my hair the way it is."

"And Paulo-Marcel, of course, is our guru of things having to do with those parts of our anatomy that sprout hair above our neck."

Cosima did not appreciate his sarcasm. "How can you be so out of touch?" she spat. "Don't you ever read W? Don't you ever read the style section in the New York Times? Honest to God, Fletch, you are a fucking idiot when it comes to women's fashion."

"*I am indeed an idiot*," he thought for subjecting myself to this. *If it weren't for the girls...*

"Puff, puff, wheeezz, puff." She was back at it.

Fletcher stared at her as she puffed and pulled and bust her butt for several minutes before she looked up at him and barked between puffs," Quit thinking!"

Again Fletcher ignored her. "You know, Cosima, I can't help thinking that if they're looking for someone to become this year's anorexia poster girl, you might want to apply."

For a moment she said nothing, letting the pressure build before, like a volcano, she erupted and spewed her molten ire on him. "Fletcher, you are an asshole. You are a sonofabitch, and I will make you pay for that remark. You are going to pay and you can go to the bank on that, you shit!" She said nothing for several minutes until she had regained some of her composure. "May I remind you of the Babe Palely axiom that, 'No woman can ever be too thin or have too many shoes.'"

"I think her quote was, 'too rich or too thin.'"

"That's even better," she spat back.

"Oh, thank God," Fletcher got up to leave the room. "You're not suffering anorexia *nervosa* after all, just *axiom absurdum*."

Metamorphosis

Though Fletcher would never have admitted it to Cosima, or to anybody else for that matter, Hildy was his favorite daughter. While Julie seemed to take an instant dislike to him the moment she emerged from the womb, Hildy, as a child, had been his little furry caterpillar that would climb into his lap before bedtime and ask him to read a story. Then at ten, she had spun herself a cocoon and refused to talk to either of her parents.

Now at twelve, the butterfly was slowly emerging from the cocoon. She had begun to show signs of approaching womanhood, and he suspected that it would only be a matter of time, a short time, that she would fly off to test her wings. He normally treasured his times alone with her, times like now, as they drove alone to school. It gave him a chance to plumb the depths of Hildy's emerging personality.

"So, what are you learning in school, these days?" Dumb question. Guaranteed to immediately irritate a twelve-year-old. It drew an obvious answer.

"Nothing."

"Nothing? Well, then I guess we won't need to pay next semester's tuition. Maybe I should get you a job as a waitress at a diner."

Her response to his attempt at humor made it clear that she was not in a mood to be trifled with. "Oh, Dad, like, get real."

Like get real? What did that mean? What did he have to do to get real? The conversation had fallen into a pothole, and it was only after several minutes of silence that Hildy decided to pull it out.

"Can I ask you a question, Dad?"

"Of course."

"Are you and Mom still ... like ... *doin' it?*"

What kind of question was that from his twelve-year-old daughter? "What do you mean?" He hoped he had either misinterpreted her question or, at the very least, his return question would give him time to muster a proper parental response.

"You know, are you still ... *doin' it?*"

Fletcher did his best to compose himself. "If I understand what you mean by *'doin' it,'* and I think I do, I have to wonder why you're asking?"

"Cause I want to know if you and Mom plan to have any more kids? We're studying reproduction in biology and learning about, you know, *doin' it.*"

Good grief. Where had the years gone? His little caterpillar was old enough to learn about *doin' it.* He'd read how today's teenagers were becoming sexually active at a younger age and, for a moment, he was tempted to ask if she was *doin' it.* Fortunately, he had the good sense to quell the urge. Hildy hadn't even been on a date, and as far as he could tell, she had not developed an active interest in boys.

"No," he said at last, "your Mom and I are happy with the two we have. There won't be any more."

"So you're not, like *doin' it* any more?"

The truth was they weren't *doin' it* anymore, but not because they were trying to avoid procreation and not because he enjoyed the celibate life. In short, it wasn't his decision as to when or where or even if they would be *doin' it* ...ever. Given Cosima's recent declaration that she wished to liberate herself from their marriage now that she had inherited her mother's considerable estate, conjugal sex seemed out of the question. But this was not the time or place to discuss the deterioration of his relationship with Cosima . He decided to change the subject.   "Are you learning about reproduction in biology?"

"No, in biology we're learning about global warming, and how we're ruining the environment by using up all the resources and leaving the rest of the world with just about nothing."

"That's what you're learning in biology?"

"Yep."

I knew that school was too extreme, he thought. *But Cosima wouldn't listen. She and I are going to have to talk about this.* He decided to probe another subject. "I saw you reading your history book the other day. Have you studied the Civil War yet?"

"Sorta ..."

"Sorta?"

"Our teacher said that the only thing we had to know was that the war freed the slaves, but not really because they are still oppressed, and that we should give them reparations." She looked up at him quizzically, "What are reparations?"

He wanted to answer, "a sham" and leave it at that. But he decided he had to come up with some type of definition. "Well, it's sort of a penalty paid to a group of people who haven't been injured by another group of people who had nothing to do with the injury the first group never had."

Hildy looked up at him blankly and said, "Oh."

He decided to continue with his probe. "What have they taught you about the Revolution?"

"The sixty's revolution?"

"The *American* Revolution." And then with a tinge of frustration he added, "The one we celebrate on the Fourth of July."

"A little, but our teacher said it was mostly about some dead white guys who aren't all that important to our lives in the 21st century."

"George Washington isn't important any more?" He asked incredulously.

"Yeah, because … I guess, like … well, Dad, he's, like, dead."

"True." It was hard to argue with absolute fact. For a moment, he began to consider how best to begin the process of deprogramming his daughter who was obviously being brainwashed by a cult of radical Bolsheviks passing themselves off as teachers at the Bountiful Country Day School. "Just out of curiosity, what does your teacher look like?"

"Mr. Sporze?"

"Is that his name, 'Sporze?'"

She nodded. "He's really cool looking."

"Cool looking?"

"Yeah, he has real long, black hair and a long braid down the middle of his back which he sometimes, like, wears wrapped around his head. He's got a beard, which is kinda scudzie."

"Scudzie?"

"It's really blotchy lookin' … like … remember when Puddy Tat had that skin disease?"

"You mean when her fur came out in handfuls?"

59

"Yeah. It sorta looks like that."

"A Bolshevik with a black, blotchy beard," he said mostly to himself. "What an appealing looking fellow he must be."

"Mr. Sporze dresses like an Indian. I mean, like, he doesn't wear a feather or anything, but he sorta looks like an Indian. But what's really cool is that he lives in the back of a great big truck."

And I'm paying for this? he asked himself. Then it occurred to him how much of an absentee father he'd been, at least since Hildy had left the Livonia public elementary school for the private day school. Overwhelmed with his job responsibilities, he had, for all practical purposes, abrogated most of his parental responsibilities and left them to Cosima. Did she condone this nihilist education or was she as ignorant as he was about what was going on in Hildy's classes?

He decided to try another tact. "What's your favorite class?"

"English."

"Oh, are you reading stories?"

"No, we're writing."

"Writing? Like what?"

"Poetry. Wanna hear one of my poems?"

"Absolutely. I'd love to."

Hildy opened up her schoolbag and sorted through some papers. "Here it is. You ready?"

Fletcher nodded and said, "Read on, Wordsworth."

Hildy laid the poem in her lap and took a moment to compose herself for the poem's premier presentation.

"I see a world of death and pain.
There is no sun, there is no rain.

The earth has turned to dust and sand,
It's all the fault of wasteful man.
Down with all of nature's foes,
Smash 'em, burn 'em, anything goes."

Fletcher was speechless and did his best to appear to be giving her work serious consideration. "Well, that's quite a statement," he said leaving out the adjective "subversive." *Who is this person next to me, he wondered? I'm taking a stranger to school.* Or had Hildy suddenly become a budding activist?

"What did you think of the poem?"

"Well ... ahhh ... everything certainly rhymes."

"Stop!" She shouted suddenly.

Fletcher jumped on the brakes. "What? Did I hit something?"

"No, I just want to get out here."

"But, we're still two blocks from school."

"I know," she said, opening the door.

"Why don't I drive you up to the front?"

She hesitated, and then, clearly hiding the truth said, "I'd just rather walk, Dad, like, if it's okay with you."

Did she have a rendezvous with a boy? Someone she planned to walk with the last two blocks? Was she going to meet some friends? Or maybe the Bolshevik with the beard? *Like* he needed to know. "Sure, it's okay with me, but I don't understand why you don't want me to drop you off at the front door?"

"Well, Dad, like, this is our clean air week and ... ahhh, my teachers know you work for a car company ... and since cars pollute ... well, it would be, like, embarrassing if they were to see me with you." Before she closed the door she leaned her head in, blew him a kiss off her fingers and said, "Love ya, Dad."

With that, she ran off to a bunch of radicals waiting to fill her mushy brain with garbage. At that moment, he made up his mind not only to become an involved parent, but an anti-activist one as well.

He watched as she joined several other girls and then turned his V8 pollution producer, this scourge of the environment, this villain of global warming toward downtown and his office. For the first time he felt totally disenfranchised from his family. Given Cosima's regular financial infusions from Centerport via her mother, not only did they no longer need him to provide the basic necessities, they didn't need him for much of anything. And Hildy, his favorite, had now fully emerged from her cocoon to become a butterfly flying solo.

Vocational Adjustment

That they had misspelled Popper Waddington's name on his retirement watch was disappointing, but not surprising. It was, in fact, a kind of left-handed tribute to his corporate longevity and his determination to remain virtually invisible so that he might slip through the years totally unnoticed by the gods of employee downsizing. During his son's formative years, he had tried to impart his personal philosophy for survival in school: "Don't sit in the front row or the back row. Those are the people who get noticed by the teacher. Sit somewhere in the middle, off to the side where they really can't see you. Blend in. Avoid eye contact. Don't volunteer. The only time you should raise your hand is when you can't wait for the bathroom break." And then when Preston got his first job, Popper offered this: "Keep a low profile, son. Keep your head down. Don't spend too much time in one place. Remember, it's hard to hit a moving target. If you think there's chance you might screw something up, pass the buck. Always be ready to pin the blame-tail on somebody else."

Several years after his retirement, Popper had an epiphany that he felt compelled to share with his son whose employment with the Cummings Manufacturing Company had begun to look tenuous, if not terminal. "In addition to all the advice I've given you about keeping a low profile, there's one more thing you need to know," Popper began, "if you want to survive in the corporate world, you've got to find a way to make yourself indispensable."

"Keep a low profile and make myself indispensable? In a company with over two thousand employees. How do I do that?"

His father smiled. "I wish I had an answer, but I'm afraid, my boy, that's something you have to figure out for yourself."

Preston Waddington did figure it out for himself, but it wasn't easy. The process began the day he felt *her* presence outside his office cubical. When he turned around and looked up, he saw an intensely thin, boney-looking woman dressed in a white blazer, with a small insignia on her breast pocket that he could not read. She wore a white skirt, white stockings, white shoes, and her hair was white, not grey-white, but silky white. Even her skin had an albino-like whiteness to it.

She smiled down at him with suspect benevolence. "My name is Felicity Truehart, and I'd like to have you pick up all your personal belongings and follow me."

She continued smiling at him, but he did not find her smile the kind of smile one would expect of someone who was about to sit down for a pleasant chat. What was it with her smile? It didn't look real. It was almost as if she'd been the victim of a bad face-lift that deadened the nerves around her mouth and left her with a ridiculous grin permanently plastered over her teeth. She repeated her instructions, "I'd like to have you pick up all your personal belongings and follow me."

"Why?" Preston asked blankly.

"That will be made clear to you in a few moments," the woman in white said.

She held out her hand in the same way she might have offered it to a small child before crossing a busy street. He stared at her fingers. They were as boney, white, and as unappetizing as the rest of her. Preston tacitly declined the offer.

"Please, just come with me, and we'll do our best to make this as painless as possible."

Painless did she say? Why are we talking about pain? He wondered.

"I'm waiting, Mr. Waddington." Her voice was now laced with impatience.

Sonnavabitch! I'm being canned. That's what this is all about. They're firing me. His stomach dropped somewhere just above his shoe tops, leaving a hollow place in his mid-section for panic to run rampant.

"We are on a schedule, Mr. Waddington." There was urgency in her voice.

"They operate like a swat team," he'd been told by a neighbor who'd been the victim of downsizing at his plastics company. "Their tactic is to sneak onto an office floor, target the victims, and then surprise 'em, strip 'em, and slip 'em out fast, before they can do any damage or alert other employees to what's going down."

"Please, just your personal things," she repeated.

The woman is a broken record, Preston thought.

"We'll take care of the rest."

"I've been fired, right?"

"Let's just say that you have been ..." She paused as if intent on finding the right term. She found one. "Vocationally Adjusted."

"Which is another way of saying I've been fired," Preston responded, making no attempt to suppress his obvious disdain for the euphemism.

"We would like you to think of this experience as being given the opportunity to reset your career horizon." The plastic surgeon's mistake remained fixed in place.

"Is there any reason the word 'fired' seems to be missing from your vocabulary?"

"It's not a pretty word," she said.

"It's not a pretty act, either," Preston retorted.

"Now, Mr. Waddington," she said, avoiding eye contact and addressing herself to a point high above his head as though she expected her words to rise, then cascade over him like a warm shower, "the first rule of successful career redirection is to adopt a positive mental attitude."

Screw a positive mental attitude. Preston was angry. What had he done to deserve this? Was this just some random act that he had fallen victim to? Or was there someone upstairs that had it in for him? He took a deep breath and stared at the desk that had been his office home for over four years. He picked up his briefcase, the picture of his wife and young daughter, a couple of books, and then glanced around to see if there was anything else he should be taking with him.

"*Just* the personal items," Felicity Truehart reminded him in a voice that did little to mask the authority she was prepared to exercise. "Try and think of this as an old door closing, and that I'm here to help you open a new door in your life."

The thought of having to face his wife with the news of his firing weighed heavily on him. The fact that he would be without a paycheck was bad enough, but first he had to endure the humiliation of having to walk past all his fellow employees knowing that they knew he was being carted off to Outplacementville.

As he left his cubicle, he felt like one of those criminals he'd seen on the television news being lead off to the police station. The *perp walk*. Only they always seemed to be carrying raincoats that they used to hide their faces. But he didn't have a raincoat. There was no cover, no way to hide his face. He would have to bear the full shame of having been selected for Vocational Adjustment. Barely a dozen steps out of his office, he realized that he didn't need a raincoat.

As Preston looked out over the sea of cubicles, he saw dozens of Felicity Truehart clones, both male and female, each delivering a personalized and smiling *coup de grace.* At least he was not alone. Blood was everywhere. It was now evident that his selection had been just the luck, the bad luck, of the downsizing draw.

The elevator carrying Felicity Truehart and Preston sank to the lowest floor in the building. To the best of his recollection, he had never ventured into the sub-basement. The woman in white was talking at Preston. Not *with* him. *At* him. He was doing his best to ignore the litany of little reassurances and simple platitudes presumably programmed into her training to help facilitate the acceptance and adjustment phase. He wanted her to stop talking. No, he wanted God to strike her dumb. And if God wouldn't accommodate him, he was prepared to take matters into his own hands. If management had intended that he direct his anger toward her, and not toward them, they were succeeding.

The elevator released them into a long, dimly lit passageway that looked foreign and strange to Preston. For a moment, he was convinced that somehow they had passed out of the building altogether. At the end of the hall, he saw double doors begin to open, slowly, filing the corridor with a bright, white light. A man appeared, silhouetted in the doorway.

Felicity Truehart stopped and moved aside, gesturing for him to continue. "I will rejoin you later," she said. Her voice was hushed, as though they had entered a funeral chapel.

As Preston approached, the man in the doorway spoke to him in the same genteel tone and manner as the woman in white. Clearly, their training involved some type of procedural cloning. "My name is Bob, and I'm here to help you through this."

"Bob? Just Bob?" Preston expected him to have a more imposing name.

"Just Bob," Bob affirmed.

Preston was immediately struck by how big Bob was. He had been handed off to what appeared to be a bar bouncer turned outplacement specialist. Preston imagined that he could, and possibly would, use his size to deal conclusively with any of those being Vocationally Adjusted who might decide to rebel or express their displeasure in some aggressive manner. Preston could not make out Bob's facial features as he was still silhouetted by the bright white light behind him. He could, however, see that Bob's head was large, and that there had been a long interval since his last visit to a barber. Preston found himself involuntarily amused that this large, faceless, hairy man was the angel assigned to escort him to the way station of unemployment. He was wrong. The Angel Bob simply pointed him into a large room filled with chairs and an assemblage of employees who had suffered the same fate as he.

It was an Ellis Island of despondent rejects. A grey cloud of humiliation hung heavy in the room. Preston noticed that a few of the people were openly voicing their anger, two were crying, and several others stared blankly at the floor. He found a seat, leaned back, and stared at the ceiling, wishing that somewhere in the acoustic tiles, he might find some answers. What now? What would he do? He had to have a paycheck. He had a mortgage, car payments, a three-year-old daughter with an asthmatic condition, and his wife was expecting their second child in less than two months. Maybe there would be severance pay, but how long would it last? To the next job?

An hour passed. Two hours. Preston looked up every time another unfortunate arrived. It wasn't long until all the chairs were filled. Those who straggled in last were resigned to sitting on the floor or holding up a wall. More time passed and he wondered why someone hadn't appeared to talk to them. Where were Felicity Truehart and the Angel Bob? Was he supposed to sign something? Meet with an outplacement specialist? Leave?

At first, he wasn't sure what it was that had been placed on his shoulder. But a quick glance revealed the pressure had come from one of Angel Bob's enormous paws. His other hand held out a folded piece of paper.

"Apparently, you will not be going on with us. Another time, perhaps, but not today." The Angel Bob sounded as if he regretted having to disappoint him.

"You've been called back." He handed him the message. "It appears a Mr. Axel McPherson has plans for you. He's a VP. He can do that."

II

Axel McPherson who was Preston's boss had brought him back from the brink. He had planned to make Preston assistant manager of the sales promotion department. Apparently, Human Resources had never seen his memo and, in their frenzy to reduce the headcount, had included Preston in the carnage.

At first, Preston was just happy to have survived the purge. He felt reasonably secure knowing that his job was protected under Axel's VP umbrella. But as more employees from various departments found themselves meeting with clones of Felicity Truehart and the Angel Bob, and as it became clear that no one's job was totally secure, Preston decided he had to find some way to protect himself. He made up his mind to take his father's advice and create an aspect of his job that was so important, so indispensable to the company as to make him immune to layoffs, budget cuts, or the caprice of some bean counter. An idea began to form and take shape in his mind ... *a plan* was born. It rolled out in front of his eyes like a red carpet bearing weekly paychecks leading all the way to retirement. And, hopefully, maybe even to a promotion. Maybe several promotions. An unobstructed route to the executive floor. *Yes! Yes! Yes! That's it!*

To implement his plan, Preston got his name inserted on the distribution list for the manufacturing division's daily production standards compliance reports. Each day, the foremen on the several production lines would record endless columns of figures and production details that would numb the faculties and stifle the discernment of even the most fanatical production manager. In truth, ninety-five percent of the information in these reports was unnecessary. Like many things in corporations, the reports had long since become part of the daily fabric. Preston organized the minutiae and numbers, reformatted the reports, and added pages of commentary, which, in reality, only restated in words that which was immediately apparent in the numbers. The result of his effort was a several hundred-page document that he titled the *Company Eyes Only* report. Soon, management referred to it simply as the *CEO*.

Preston was sure that someone would see the CEO for what it was and a clone of Felicity Truehart would knock at his cubicle and send him to outplacementville. Months passed and no knock came. He continued to look for ways to enhance his report.

He decided it would add impact if he had a large rubber stamp made with red ink that read: "*Private Information---Approved Distribution List Only.*" Soon to be included on the *CEO* distribution list, became a status symbol that the chosen managers who could point to their copy of the CEO as one more testament to their importance. So highly regarded was his publication that upper management moved him up four floors, gave him an office with a door, a raise and assigned him a secretary.

As time went by and no one questioned what he was doing, or why, or even who had authorized the publication, he began to add reports and documents from other departments - marketing, sales, finance. Within less than two years, virtually everyone in the company assumed that copies of all documents and reports, whatever the subject, should be sent to Preston.

Once all the information was in Preston's hands, he would sort and sift and evaluate for inclusion. His monthly reports were masterpieces of dull reading. He worked hard to be sure that it would be literally impossible for any of those on the distribution list to read more than the first page without having their eyes glaze over. Unlike most people who create reports, Preston's goal was not to inspire praise for the content, but to create awe at the poundage. He understood that the larger the document, the greater its perceived importance, but the lower its actual readership. The last thing he wanted was for someone to read, *really* read, the *CEO* for fear they might begin to ask questions: "Do we really need this?" or "Aren't we wasting a lot of paper duplicating reports we already have? Should the company be wasting its time on this?" Yes, a perceptive reader could have well been his undoing. But the odds were against that ever happening. One thing Preston had learned during his years with the corporation: The company was long on egos, but short on perceptive readers.

During the third year of the *CEO*'s publication, he conceived a *truly* brilliant idea. He decided to add a summary page to the front of the report. It proved to be a masterstroke. As he explained to his father during a visit to Sun City, "You're an executive and a report crosses your desk. What's the one thing you'd really like to see in that summary?"

"That the company is making money," seemed to be the most obvious answer to his father.

"That's secondary. What you really want to see is ... *your name*. But only if it's associated with something positive, praiseworthy, or even heroic. When people see their names praised in a report, they feel good about themselves and more importantly, they feel good about the person who put their name there in the first place."

That was the essence and brilliance of his summary page. Preston never found fault, never criticized, never questioned production decisions or noted declines in productivity or sales. He made sure his reports praised, lauded, commended, complemented, and extolled leadership. He created high profile heroes of dozens of men, if not in the eyes of their underlings who knew better, at least in the summary pages of his report.

His success with the CEO aside, he nevertheless lived in fear that his bogus publication would be exposed. One day, the company president, Charles Fair came to him with a complement and a suggestion. He loved the *Company Eyes Only*. "But wouldn't it be an even better publication if each monthly report contained a note, a quote, and a pithy bit of industry insight from the president?"

Talk about validating the weekly report and assuring its longevity. Preston was more than happy to accommodate him. The *Fair Opinion* from the company's president became a featured segment in *Company Eyes Only*. The president's sycophants loved it. And, Preston was told, so did members of the board of directors. Charlie decided to move Preston up to the executive floor and give him a raise and VP title.

Charlie also made a point at one of his quarterly management meeting to declare that the CEO report was an *indispensable* component of inner company communications. And by inference, so was its creator.

Preston's salary was now well into the low six figures all of which made it possible for him to move from Eastport to Centerport. He was given a key to the executive men's room. He ate his lunches in the executive dining room where he was treated with great deference by the other executives, especially when they found their name on the top page of the monthly CEO. Years passed and the CEO remained an unchallenged fixture. Maybe he would never be found out.

III

It was five years later that Charlie Fair was found drown in his French maid's bath tub. At first it was classified as an accident. Later, when all the facts were in and confessions made, it turned out to be second degree murder. As it turned out it might never have happened if Charlie had shot his regular round of golf that fateful Saturday. But he had not. He had carded his one and only eighteen-hole par.

His smile had begun on the eighteenth green at the Centerport Country Club and was still frozen on his face as he drove home. "A 72! A par, goddamn it," he said aloud to no one but himself. His drives had split the fairways; he had reached all but two greens in regulation, and his putts had eyes. "Fuckin' eyes." Never in thirty years had he had such a day on the golf course.

To make things even better, he had cleaned the clocks of his foursome for $500. Life was good. *Very* good. Not only on the golf course, but at the office as well. Yes, everything was under control. *Damn! I've got to frame this scorecard,* he thought. As he entered his house, he found Flaubert, the butler, in the kitchen. "Is Mrs. Fair here?" He asked.

"No, sir, she went out about eleven. I imagine she'll be home around five."

"Five?" He looked at his watch. Three hours. His eyes drifted up in the direction of the apartment over his garage where the Fair's two French maids slept. A total French massage, he decided, would be a proper reward for his triumph on the golf course. He hurried up the stairs to the maid's quarters.

"Hello, Jeanette," Charlie said as he opened her bathroom door and found her up to her neck in fluffy bubbles. *Good grief,* he thought, *the woman seems to spend most of her time in the bathtub. She might not be more than an average housekeeper, but she certainly keeps herself clean.*

"Monsieur Fair. Have you come to visit Jeanette?"

"Yes, I have," he said enthusiastically.

"It has been some weeks since you visit me. I thought you might be visiting Monique," she said referring to the other French maid.

"No, I came to see you."

"She is a tart, you know?"

"Who? Monique?"

"She sleeps with the new gardener."

"She does?" Charlie found the idea of Monique rolling in one of the flowerbeds with the gardener very funny.

"No class, that one."

"And who do you sleep with?"

"I sleep alone," she said tossing her head defiantly.

"Have you got room in there for me?" He knew, of course, that she would not refuse him.

"You are the master. You can do what you want."

"I want what you want."

"Well, I suppose I would like you to join me." She sat up so that her breasts were above the bubble line.

Charlie needed no further invitation. He quickly undressed, carefully hanging his slacks and polo shirt on a towel rack and slipped into the tub.

"Ah, the water is perfect. The same as your body temperature, I presume."

"You had a nice golf game?"

"I had a spectacular golf game, thank you. And I can think of no better reward for having played so well than spending an hour or two with you."

"Two hours in the tub?"

"No, five minutes here, two hours in your bed."

Suddenly Jeanette's face turned ashen and she sank quickly below the bubbles.

"Well, don't we look comfortable," his wife said.

"Olivia! It's not five. I thought you were..." Charlie briefly considered joining Jeannette under the cover of the bubbles. The only practical option was to immediately mount his defense with a denial, "This is not what it looks like."

"No? Well, let's see, what does it look like? Maybe it looks like you're here because your tub is not working, and I know how you love bubble baths. Or maybe it looks like this tub for two is part of your effort to conserve water. Or could it look like something else?"

"You've got this all wrong. I was coming up for a massage and … well, I hadn't taken a shower after golf." *God that sounded lame*, he thought.

"And you wanted to be extra clean for Jeanette. How considerate." She stared at the end of the tub where Jeanette had remained submerged. "Do you think she plans to surface again? Or should we just let her drown?"

Charlie started to pull himself out of the tub.

"Please, Charlie, don't get out of the tub on my account. But do plan to get out of the house on my account in the next two hours. And you can take Jeannette with you. Tomorrow you may call with the address of where you'll be staying. Flaubert will see to it that all your clothes and personal items are delivered there."

"What are you talking about?"

"I'm talking about divorce. You'll be getting the papers at your new address from my lawyer on Monday."

"Olivia. You're upset. Let's talk about this after you've calmed down."

"Talk? Well, that would be a new dimension in our relationship."

"I'm your husband. You can't just throw me out."

"I don't intend to throw you anywhere. You will walk out under your own power or I'll have the sheriff help you leave."

"Now hold on, Olivia."

"Hold on? To what? My house? Oh, yes, I'll hold on to my house and most of what's in it. I'll also hold on to my trust. All of it. Good-bye, Charlie. It has been less than a pleasure living with you." With that she turned quickly and left.

Charlie sat stunned in the bubble bath that had all but reduced itself to a soapy film on top of the water.

Suddenly a gasping French truffle broke the surface and, in what seemed to be one unbroken motion, jumped up, "Is Mrs. Fair going to fire me?"

"Consider yourself fired," Charlie said flatly.

"No notice?"

"No notice."

"Where will we go?" she was nearing tears.

Charlie looked up at her with an incredulous expression. "What do you mean 'we?'"

She barely took a breath before she unleashed her anger both verbally and physically. Vous merde! Vous bâtard misérable ! Vous fils de pute! she screamed as she slammed the extra large economy size glass bottle of bubble bath hard on Charlie's head. Slowly her unconscious employer sank beneath the bubbles.

IV

The company was now without a president. After a week of requisite corporate mourning, the board met to consider his replacement and announced that during their search they intended to clean house, to cut the fat out of their expenses and to eliminate all non essential jobs and activities. Preston was sure that they were finally on to him and his CEO. If ever there was a useless document, that had to be it. From his office on the executive floor he had a direct view of the boardroom door. Emma Rae Sharpe who had been Charlie Fair's secretary was now, apparently, serving as messenger to the condemned. He watched as again and again she would leave the floor and return with a manager who had been slated by the board to have his head lopped off. Without Charlie's protection, Preston was sure he was on the list. Days passed, heads rolled, changes were made. Finally, word came that he was to wait in his office and that at ten o'clock Emma Rae would come for him.

Preston waited. Ten o'clock came and went. Emma Rae had not moved from her desk. Eleven. Quarter to twelve. He began to wonder if they'd forgotten about him. Maybe he should ask Emma Rae. No, bad idea. She'd tell him nothing Truth was that she hated him since the day he discovered Charlie and her engaged in flagrante delicto on Charlie's office couch. She seemed to regard his discovery as a shameless intrusion and made it clear to Preston that she would, one day, avenge what she considered a personal affront. He looked at his watch. It was almost twelve-thirty.

The board room doors opened and someone came out and said something to Emma Rae who immediately looked in his direction. His time had come. The moment of truth. The defining moment between what was past and what was yet to be. Had he let his overactive, well-honed sense of corporate reality get the best of him? Had he worried himself into a state of near mental anorexia for no reason? Maybe, he found himself hoping, all they wanted was to give him information to be included in the next CEO. They said they liked it. Or had he read the tea leaves of uncertainty correctly? He was to be axed. In a few moments, he would walk across the foyer, pass through the double doors, and take a seat at the foot of the teak conference table. There he would look across the polished expanse at the solemn faces of the executive committee. Would their expressions be stern, sympathetic, resolute? Preston was betting on the latter. After some perfunctory explanation, he would be asked if he would be so kind to place his head in the corporate chopping block and let them sever both his head and the Company Eyes Only from the corporate ledger

Emma Rae stood up and started toward him. He could write the script: She would come into his office, greet him with a malevolent smile, and say something flip and nasty like, "You drew the short straw, asshole! Or "Times up, shithead!" Or maybe she would decide to say something really ugly, like, "I hope they start by smashing your nuts in a vice." Emma Rae was capable of extraordinary verbal cruelty.

Preston turned and stared out the window, as if by turning his back on the approaching Emma Rae, he would prolong the inevitable. He heard her knock on the doorframe. Preston turned. There were tears in her eyes. *For me?* he wondered. Good heavens. Could she, at this eleventh hour, have developed a sense of compassion? It was hard to believe. Emma Rae dabbed at her eyes, "Allergies," she mumbled and then looked at him with the same disdain she might have shown had she caught him relieving himself in his potted plant.

They trod over the lush, blue Stark carpet with its corporate logo. The heavy, mahogany floor-to-ceiling boardroom doors loomed large in front of him. Emma Rae veered off toward her desk leaving him standing alone before the portals. She looked back at him as if hoping he'd trip over the doorsill and fall on his face in front of the executive committee.

Emma Rae gestured with her left hand toward the door, as if to say, "There's the door handle schmuck; use it." Preston extended his hand toward the large, polished, brass handle with the ornate grape vine motif on the faceplate. The metal felt cold to the touch. His fingers rested for a moment before they began to tighten. Slowly they complied with his command, though they seemed reluctant to fully affix themselves with any degree of firmness. Finally, he had the handle full in his grasp.

Preston opened the door and saw before him the Board of Directors. *What's this?* They were smiling. The Chairman stood up and held out his hand.

"We need somebody in the president's office who knows what's going on in the company. Somebody with his finger on manufacturing, marketing, sales and finance. We decided that no one knows more of what's going in the company than someone who for the last several years has been indispensable."

Who would that be? Preston wondered.

"That person, of course, is you. The board has decided that you should be our President."

Preston was stunned. He had come in prepared to have them hand him his head and instead they wanted to hand him the presidency. *Are they nuts?* he thought. *I'd have to manage two thousand people and I can't even manage my kids. To be fair to the company, I've got to say no. I'm not qualified.*

The chairman handed him a piece of paper outlining his compensation package. It spelled out his salary, his stock options, the company limo, paid vacations, access to the company plane and all the other perks he would receive. It was a heady offer. *With this we could buy an even larger house in Centerport*, he thought. But that was followed by a more sobering question, *Do I really want to answer to a board of directors that is so misguided, so ill-advised, so myopic as to make someone as unqualified as me the president?* He looked again at the bottom line of the compensation package. *This is uber territory*, he realized. His eyes glazed over, his forehead began to sweat, his hands shook, his heart pounded. It was more a reflex response than a considered acceptance when he said," I'm your guy."

No sooner were the words out than he found himself asking, *What if the company loses money? What if there's a product recall? Who are they going to blame? I could quickly go from indispensable to dispensable. How do I survive?* The answer came to him as he remembered the advice his father had given him so many years ago. "Keep a low profile, son. Keep your head down. Don't spend too much time in one place. Remember, it's hard to hit a moving target. If you think there's a chance you might screw something up, pass the buck. Always be ready to pin the blame-tail on somebody else."

Five years later, Preston had not only survived as president, he'd written a NY Times best seller on management survival techniques - Waddington's Wisdom - with a forward by Jack Welch, and had appeared three times on the Cavuto on Business TV show.

The Best of Enemies

Max watched the naked woman walk out of the sea. At least to him she momentarily appeared to be naked. She was wearing a white, one-piece bathing suit that had become virtually transparent in the water - a tribute to the marvels of fiber chemistry. At first Max was embarrassed for her, but that was quickly replaced with the carnal appetite of a twenty-one-year young man's desire to see more.

As she walked up on the Centerport beach, he was fascinated by the way she tossed her head back giving her long silken hair the freedom to blow free in the wind. He marveled at the way she moved with easy, even strides across the sand to the place where she'd spread her beach blanket. She didn't sit down, but rather, it seemed to Max, glided onto the blanket with a gracefulness and control any fashion model would have envied. Max wasn't sure if he was feeling lust or love, but whichever it was, it undulated with unfiltered passion through his body.

"Who the hell is that fantastic piece of pulchritude?" his friend Robby asked as he sat down next to Max on the mosaic of beach towels they'd laid out.

"I've never seen her before," Max answered, his eyes straining against the glare off the water.

"You can see everything!" Robby exclaimed.

"And there's a lot of everything to see," Max added appreciatively.

"Boy, if that isn't an invitation to a dance, I've never seen one."

"A dance?" Max teased. "You want to take her to a dance? You go dancing; I have other places I'd like to take her." Max picked up his towel and the ice chest with the beer and scrambled to his feet.

"Where are you going?" Robby asked.

"I don't like the sand here or the company," he said with mock seriousness and then started to make his way through the clusters of bodies, towels, and beach umbrellas between himself and the see-through bathing suit.

"You're gonna need some expert help with that," Robby said following on his heels.

"Does Jordan Spieth need help on the golf course? Why don't you go play in the sand for awhile?" He knew Robby would ignore him, but at least he was determined to get the jump on him.

"I would, but I forgot my shovel and pail," Robby retorted as he jumped in front of Max, taking the lead in their cross-beach quest.

Their hair was light from the sun, their skins a smooth bronze. Their bodies were athletically hard and the muscles in their flat stomachs rippled like heavy ropes They were both the issue of substantial Centerport families and were currently between their junior and senior years at Yale. Both boys' parents had suggested they might want to think about getting a summer job. They agreed...to *think* about it. Robby did give it some thought and decided summer work was not for him. Max managed to get a part-time job as a waiter with a catering company which needed him for only a few nights a week leaving his days free for the beach.

Each day Max led them down to the beach to bask in the female ogles. Max knew what was on the minds of the doe-eyed younger ones, but he had neither the insight nor experience to understand the meaning behind the subtle scrutiny, the appreciative gazes cast on them by the 'older women' - the prospective Mrs. Robinsons. All he truly understood, and this mostly intuitively, was that their youth and bodies gave them title to the beach and that summer was harvest time.

As Max approached the girl in the see-through bathing suit, he felt a surge of fleshy excitement watching her apply tanning lotion to her inner thighs. His mind danced off to a concupiscent fantasy in which he saw himself performing that particular service for her. He quickly abandoned the tenuous fantasy bubble as he saw Robby flick out his towel and let it settle next to her blanket. Quickly Max sat down on the other side of the woman and immediately the assault began.

"I'm from the official beach welcoming committee," Robby said seizing the initiative. "My name is Robby Trask." He paused a moment glancing at Max and then let his eyes wander back to her face by way of the nipples which were still on prominent display under the wet suit. He leaned close to her as if to avoid Max hearing, "And that?" He nodded toward Max. "Well, if we ignore him maybe he'll go away."

"I'm Max Roarke," Max said moving closer so that he was now sitting by her feet. Immediately he had to check the urge to lay a hand on her leg.

She looked at him and smiled broadly, "And I'm

Andrea Francis."

"We'll have to be careful of him," Max said with a look of dead earnest as he glanced at Robby. "He hasn't been out of the juvenile correction home all that long and they tend to get a little randy when you take 'em off saltpeter."

"Humor him, Andrea," Robby injected moving closer and touching her shoulder, "it's all part of his therapy." He looked over at Max and snapped his fingers. "Now, be a good boy and show us you do have some manners after all. Offer Andrea a beer."

Max dug into the ice chest, pulled out a can, opened it, and handed it to her, "My only regret is that it isn't champagne," he said with gallant aplomb.

"Thank you," she said, obviously pleased at the attention from both of her instant suitors.

Max reached back into the chest, pulled out another, opened it, and offered it to Robby. Just as Robby was about to take it, Max's hand closed like a vice around the aluminum can forcing the beer to gush onto Robby.

"Sorry," Max said with hollow sincerity, "I forget my own strength sometimes."

Robby remained in total control and shook his head sadly as he took the deformed can from Max. Slowly his eyes met hers and in a low tone said,

"It's a tragic case. He has the body of a bull, but the mind of a tractor."

Andrea was unable to suppress a giggle.

"Now back to business," Robby said. "In order for you to obtain your certified beach pass you have to be able to answer 'yes' and 'eight o'clock' to the following question."

"Yes and eight o'clock?" she had no idea what Robby was talking about.

"Are you free tonight and what time do I pick you up?"

"You'll have to excuse Robby if he seems to come on a little fast. You see, he realizes once you get to know him there's no way you'll say 'yes.'" Max found himself wishing he could simply make Robby evaporate. As that, he knew, was not a possible option, he decided his best strategy was to change the subject. "Do you live in Southampton?"

"No, I'm from Georgetown in Washington. I'm just here for the summer visiting my aunt Petula Poor. That's her house down there," she said pointing to one of the large mansions just off the beach. "My mother is spending the summer interviewing replacements for my father."

"Recently divorced?" Robby asked.

"Officially just a year, but she's been working on it forever," Andrea said.

"You sound a mite bitter," Max observed.

"I happen to love my father. My mother gave him a raw deal."

There was a moment of awkward silence when no one seemed to know what to say or where to take the conversation. Max sensed that any more talk about her parents could very easily derail his quest to win her for the evening. Then Robby appeared to make a discovery. "You're a Virgo, right?"

Andrea's face lit up. "Right! August 26th. I'll be ... ahh.., I'll be twenty-one. How did you know I was a Virgo?" She was obviously impressed.

"I just knew. All the signs where there. I'm

sensitive to people's aura and yours is definitely Virgo."

Max could see Robby had scored some significant points with a lucky guess and he bit back a sudden urge to shout 'bullshit' and moved to neutralize the impact Robby's Virgo guess had had on her. With all the objectivity of a casual observer he said, "If I remember correctly, that's the first time your birth sign ploy has worked for you, isn't it Robby?"

"You guys are just too much!" she laughed. "Do you always go at each other like this?"

"Only when the favors of a beautiful woman are at stake," Robby said.

The harmless give and take went on with only occasional respite for another half hour. Max worked to check Robby's pointed gibes to protect the inroads he felt he had made with Andrea. Finally, Max brought them back to the primary objective.

"The big question still to be answered," Max said, "is which one of us are you going out with tonight?"

"Are you both asking me?"

"We're both asking," Max replied. "But we expect you to choose only one of us. Maybe I ought to rephrase the question to give you a better perspective: Do you want to go out for dinner and dancing with a suave, good-looking, very cultured young man like myself, or ..." he paused, took a deep breath and followed with a long sigh, "or, do you want to endanger your good name and reputation by being seen on the street with him?"

"Andrea," Robby countered, "before you decide, I think you should know that Max here ... well, how should I put it?" Robby seemed to be struggling for a tactful explanation, then appeared to give up. "The truth," he said in what Max read as mock embarrassment, "the truth be told, and I'm afraid it must be told, is that Max spends an inordinate amount of time in the shower room at the "Y" with young boys."

Low blow, Max thought. *I'd really like to wipe that smirk off his fuckin' face.* Anger began to leak up like acid reflux. Immediately he fought it back knowing that if he lost his cool he'd lose any chance of impressing Andrea. He decided to turn Robby's fabrication about boys in the shower room to his advantage. The look on his face and his body language said he was stepping back from the competitive banter. Max did his best to sound both serious and embarrassed for his friend, "I must apologize for Robby. That he's crass is pitiable; that he's uncouth is unforgivable. Not the kind of talk one would expect in front of someone like you."

Robby did his best to defect Max's apology, "I'm sorry Max," he said nesting his retort in a playful laugh, "I know how the truth hurts."

Andrea could not contain her laughter. "You two are crazy. I mean you're really crazy!"

I better lighten up, Max thought. "See what you've done to us? You've driven us crazy," Max ran his fingers playfully along the inside of her foot.

"How long have you two been friends?" She asked.

"Let's see," Max said. "We've been friends for six years."

"And enemies for eight," Robby added.

"What? Friends for six, enemies for eight?" she echoed. "How do you explain that?"

"It's a classic case," Max explained, "of 'the enemy of my enemy becoming my friend.' We both went to Amberly Prep and instantly hated each other. Then, at the start of our junior year we had an altercation."

"He means we had a fight," Robby said.

"But not with fists," Max clarified, "with the fire hoses on the third floor of our dorm."

"Turned out that old Heap didn't like the idea of water running down two flights of stairs making like it was Niagara Falls.

"Who was old Heap?" she asked.

"That's what we called the Amberly Headmaster," Max said. "We named him that because he reminded us of Uriah Heap in Dickens' David Copperfield. Like Heap, Mr. Perkins was tall, lanky and when he walked, he looked as if none of the parts wanted to move in the same direction."

"Anyway," Robby injected, "Heap decides that the only fitting punishment, short of expulsion, was to make us his indentured servants."

"How did he do that?"

"Every day after class, we had to report to his house and pick up dog poop in his back yard."

Andrea could not contain herself and began to laugh.

"He had four ... count 'em, four big dogs," Max said holding his hand about three feet off the ground to indicate their size.

"Big dogs that made big poops."

"That sounds like an awful punishment."

"No, no," Max protested with feigned sincerity, "The poop patrol was a significant character enhancing experience. And for that reason, we decided that we had to find some way to show our appreciation to Heap for the hours he permitted us to roam around his back yard looking for dog turds." Both Max and Robby could not hold back throaty guffaws.

"How did you show your appreciation?" she asked.

Max moved close to her as if about to reveal a dark secret. In that moment he felt that he could kiss her and she would not object. He managed to stop himself short of her mouth and turned to whisper in her ear, "On the night before graduation, which was scheduled for nine the next morning, we snuck into his house and Superglued his bedroom door shut."

Robby added, "And we left the phone off the hook in his den so that he couldn't call anyone from his bedroom. Next morning, everybody shows up for the ceremony and there's no Heap."

"And the graduation?" Andrea asked.

"Went on without him," Max said. "About eleven, someone decided to go looking for him. They had to call the fire department to chop down his door."

"Did he ever find out that you were the ones that had glued him in?" "Not until we told him," Robby said.

"You told him?" Andrea started to laugh. "You actually told him?"

"Well, we knew he wasn't going to rest until he found out who did it," Max said. "And we certainly didn't want Heap giving the credit to someone else. So, about a week after we left campus, when there was nothing he could do to us, we sent him a present."

"What kind of present?" She asked.

"A box of empty Superglue tubes and a dried, hard-as-a rock doggy souvenir from his backyard. And that's how we became friends." Max said proudly.

"But," Robby injected, "when it comes to which of us is going to take you out tonight, we are still mortal enemies. Which is it?"

Andrea shook her head and grinned, "As I said, you're both really crazy. But I like 'crazy.' However, as far as which of you takes me out tonight, I can't make a choice with you both sitting here. Why don't you flip a coin or something?"

Robby shook his head, "Naw, that's no good. Flipping a coin would leave it to luck."

"You got a better idea?" Max asked.

"How about some kind of contest?" Robby suggested, his mind spinning through a list of possibilities. "If there was ever a prize worth competing for, it's sitting right here." He exchanged a private prurient look with Max.

"We could wrestle," Max offered, hoping that Robby would be fool enough to accept. "NCAA rules, best two out of three falls."

Robby's face melted into a wry smile. "Now that is a truly sportsmanlike challenge coming from a guy who is Ivy League champion in his weight class."

"Okay, think of something else."

Robby's face lit up. Max guessed that his friend had come up with what he obviously believed to be an extraordinary idea.

"Given the fair damsel who is to be the prize, the contest must be the essence of chivalry," Robby said.

"Which is ...?" Max asked.

"A joust?" Andrea and Max echoed in disbelief.

"Yep. A motorcycle joust. We'll get our Kawasaki's, bring 'em down here to the beach and try to knock each other off."

"And for lances we'll use sharp sticks," Max said sarcastically, fully intending to ridicule Robby's suggestion and to underscore the very real chance of inflicting serious pain. "Tell you what; you keep on thinking up great ideas like that while Andrea and I take a walk down the beach. If we don't come back, wait here anyway."

"Well, if you're chicken ..." Robby taunted.

"Listen, if we have a joust one of us will end up skewered like a beef kabob." Robby started to sell. Max saw that the idea had captured his imagination.

"Hear me out. My mother bought a couple of big Orientals the other day and they came rolled up on these long cardboard cylinders. They're hollow, about three inches round and ten feet long. They'd make perfect lances. And because I don't want you to suffer more than just abject humiliation when I plant my lance in your chest, we'll strap boxing gloves to the ends of the cylinders."

"Where are you going to get boxing gloves?"

"Leave that to me."

Max was not surprised that he immediately found himself contemplating the pleasure of humiliating Robby by knocking him on his ass in front of Andrea.

"Come on, chicken liver," Robby taunted. "No way you can get hurt ..." he paused and a grin slipped across his lips, "... much!"

Andrea looked first at one boy, then the other. It was almost as if they'd forgotten she was even there, so intent was their attention on the joust. "Hey, she said, "Have you forgotten I'm here?"

"Forgotten?" Robby said expansively, "How could we forget our trophy?"

"You mean me?" she asked her eyes dancing with delight.

"Absolutely," Max said. As he stared into her face he realized that love and lust had become allies. He wanted her in every way possible. And if it took winning a joust to capture the incredible trophy sitting in front of him, then losing was not an option.

"I've never been a trophy before."

"There's a first time for everything," Robby said finding an excuse to touch her arm and slowly move it to her back. He turned to Max, "So, are we on?"

Max nodded and stared intently at Robby. Not only did he want to win a date with Andrea, but he was determined to knock the cocky Robby off his bike and, at the same time, punish him…to actually hurt him. Why? Just for just being Robby, who at this moment he didn't like very much. "You're on, Sir Lunch-a-lot."

Max watched as Robby's face exploded with a look of exuberant satisfaction. He knew exactly what Robby was thinking; that he'd suckered him into a mano a mano he felt sure he could win. The anticipation of combat with his friend surged through Max's body leaving a sweetness in his mouth. Boy did he want to clean Robby's clock. He'd ride the sonofabitch into the sea if he had to. No way was he going to lose this thing.

"Wait here," Robby said to Andrea, "we'll be right back. You're going to love watching what I'm going to do to Max."

II

Within twenty minutes, they returned to the beach on their motorcycles, each wearing a football helmet and shoulder pads and each carrying a long, narrow cardboard cylinder - with boxing gloves affixed to each end - which they held under their arms like jousting lances. They rode slowly across the beach, past the rows of bathers surprised to see the sudden appearance of two motorcycles. Fully intending to impress the object of their combat, they roared back and forth at the water's edge several times, gunning their engines, purposely steering through the receding waves sending up white fantails in their wakes. Finally stopped in front of Andrea on the water's edge where the sand was flat and firm,

Max noticed that Robby exuded a smug confidence and appeared to fully relish the attention Andrea and the others who had gathered were showering on him. *Enjoy it now, asshole*, Max thought as he moved closer to Andrea. *Let's see how cocky you look when you're eatin' sand.* As Max looked around at the gathering spectators, he realized the joust was taking on the trappings of a major event.

"Let's do it," Robby shouted over the sound of his engine. "First guy off his bike loses."

"You want to concede now before I embarrass you?" Max did his best to appear to be savoring the challenge and to project a cool confidence. At the same time, he began to wonder what kind of madness had he'd let himself be talked into.

Robby responded with a derisive, "Sheee-it! This isn't even going to be a contest." A thought occurred to him. "Wait a minute, I almost forgot. We've got to do this thing right." He turned off his engine and called to Andrea.

"Andrea, since you're what this joust is all about, I think it's only right that you do the honors." Robby reached into his pocket and pulled out a blue silk handkerchief. "When you drop this, the joust begins."

Andrea looked at both of them with concern, "Are you sure you aren't going to hurt yourselves?"

Robby answered with an extravagant bow, "M'lady, the prize is worth the pain."

"And pain will be the only prize he gets today," Max added.

"Ok, but don't go too fast, Okay?" she said.

Max pointed his lance at Robby, "Just fast enough to put him on his keister, which I will be doing shortly," he said in an effort to impress Andrea.

Max realized that Robby had heard his boast.

"Better say it all now, Maxie-baby," Robby shouted," because in a few minutes you're going to be on your ass."

Robby rode his motorcycle down the beach. Max turned his in the opposite direction for about fifty yards, then came to a stop by performing a neat "J" turn. What was this he was feeling? Excitement? No, it was fear. "This is nuts," he said under his breath.

"This is really nuts." Getting hit with the blunt end of the tube - boxing glove or not – could hurt a hell of a lot, especially if we're both closing at thirty miles an hour.

Andrea dropped the handkerchief and the two bikes started off, gaining speed quickly. Max found he was having difficulty holding his cardboard lance steady while maintaining control of his motorcycle. Robby looked to be having the same problem. Max passed Robby well to the right and both lances missed their marks by a wide margin. Max road back to the start, reset himself and waited for Robby to do the same. Andrea picked up the handkerchief and dropped it again. The sound of the revving engines rose above the crashing waves. Max could see that they were going to pass much closer this time. He could also see his lance was going to miss badly. In an effort to adjust his aim, he inadvertently opened himself to Robby's lance caught him on the right arm. A bolt of pain ripped through Max's shoulder forcing his hand off the throttle. For a moment, he thought he might lose control of his bike. But the sudden deceleration and the braking action of the wet sand gave him time to put his feet down and avoid toppling over.

Once again they set themselves. Max's arm hurt and he wanted to rub it. *Can't do it*, he thought. *Can't let Robby think he's hurt me. That would give the bastard too much satisfaction.* He'd let it throb. As he waited for Andrea to retrieve the handkerchief which had sailed off in a gust of wind, he decided the trick to jousting was to sucker the opponent. Max recalled how a good boxer will drop his guard, appearing to open himself to an opponent's jab, then to counter with a right cross when the other boxer has committed himself. All at once he knew exactly what he had to do.

Andrea dropped the handkerchief and they both began to accelerate. Max sat up high on his seat, purposely giving Robby a big and tempting target. At the same time, he made it appear as if he'd lost control of his lance. He could see that Robby had taken the bait and was aiming directly at Max's chest. Slowly Max rotated his lance so that it was virtually perpendicular to his motorcycle. Too late Robby realized what was happening. Max dropped forward, hugging the bike, taking away the target. Robby found himself heading straight into the broadside of Max's cylinder. It was like being hit with a swinging gate. Max passed by and then turned back to see his friend let go of the handles and his feet fly up in the air. For a long moment Robby desperately tried to balance himself like a trick rider on top of the seat. His arms and legs flailed desperately as he tried to regain control and avoid the inevitable. *No way*, Max thought. He watched as the front wheel of Robby's motorcycle veered sharply toward the ocean tumbling him off and into the water.

Max threw up his arms in victory, turned his motorcycle around and rode back to Robby who was on his knees taking off his helmet and wiping the wet sand off his face.

As Max looked at Robby he almost felt sorry for his fallen foe. But not so sorry as to resist taking a final shot at his friend, "Since you now have the night free, you can stay home and watch the Mets on the tube. Losers love company." With that, Max claimed his trophy, helping Andrea settle in behind him on the bike.

Max started off across the beach in the direction of her aunt's house.

Robby stood up and yelled, "Come back here you asshole! If you were any kind of man you'd make it two out of three!"

No sooner were the words out his mouth than Max lifted a fist high over his head and flipped a solitary finger skyward.

His Tower of Delight

The showroom floor that morning at Jack Poor Motors in Centerport was deader than road-kill until *she* walked in.

"My God," one salesman blurted impulsively as his feet fell off his desk. She's right out of a <u>Victoria's Secret</u> catalogue.

She was leggy, five-nine to five-ten, balanced confidently atop five-inch spiked heels. She had long ashen blond hair that fell with a planned carelessness over twin orbs that rose invitingly above the top of her low-cut mini blouse. The blouse itself looked as if the blouse-maker had run out of fabric at about her belly button. Her short, white leather skirt had all the inherent properties of shrink-wrap. This was not the type of customer any of the five salesmen on the floor ever expected to see in their showroom. Down the street at the Beemer or Benz dealerships, maybe. But not here.

"Who's up is it?" *(Translation: Car salesmen's parlance for whose turn is it to wait on a customer.)* The question came from a salesman on the opposite side of the sales floor as he sprang from his chair and adjusted his tie.

"Fuck whose up it is," Spud Kapock, the sales manager said. "She's mine."

Barely noticed as she paraded her package of pulchritude across the showroom in the direction of the overpriced Verite 300 sports coupe was Alfie Swenson, a fiftyish, slightly balding man who trailed slightly behind her like a dog out for its morning walk. He stood a good four inches shorter than his tower of delight and wore the apparel and jewelry adornments of a man on the downhill side of a mid-life crisis, making a last stab at reaffirming his virility. His beige cashmere sport coat, the open-collar blue shirt with just a hint of chest hair showing, the heavy gold-plated chains around his neck, the gold Patek Philippe on his wrist, and Bruno Magli shoes suggested that he could more than afford the eye-candy at his side. It also spoke loudly to what she saw in him.

"Welcome to Jack Poor Motors," Kapock said, extending his hand to Alfie, but taking advantage of the opportunity to let his eyes accept the invitation offered by the woman's attire. "My name is Spud Kapock. What can I do for you today?"

"I'm Florence," the woman volunteered in a high-pitched, baby doll-like voice. She held out her hand to Swenson. "We're here to buy a car."

"I knew right away you weren't here to buy a boat," he joked. She gave him an uncomprehending and confused look. Alfie, who got the joke, didn't laugh. *Oops*, Spud thought. *Not good. Sales train just jumped the track. Get it back, quick.* "Well, what might I show you today?"

Alfie, who had the nervous impatience of a dog in heat, spoke rapidly and intently. "I'd like to buy that Verite 300." Alfie pointed to the silver sports car sitting in the middle of the showroom floor. "That one. Right there. As it sits. And I want to drive it outta here in the next thirty minutes."

Jack Poor–*the* Jack Poor whose name was splashed all over the exterior and interior of the dealership - had been on his way down to the floor to harangue his sales force for the lack of sales activity. Gravity had not been kind to Jack Poor. In his fifties, it had pulled what were once broad shoulders and a trim waist into something that more resembled a pear. The part in his black hair had widened from a thin line to a six-inch barren landing strip. He attempted to cover it by letting his hair grow long on the left side of his head and then combing it over to the right. To keep the comb-over in place, he used a heavy jell that left his head looking as if he'd stood too close to a lube job. By the time he was sixty, his face, like his body, had drifted south, with fat filling his jowls like saddlebags. His mustache was scruffy as though his razor had malfunctioned for the last several days. Now, at sixty-seven, he looked every bit the satirical treatment one might expect from a cartoonist drawing the classic nail-their-shoes-to-the-floor-and-squeeze-the-weasels-for-every-nickel-they've-got car dealer.

Jack recognized Alfie Swenson as one of the newer Centerport residents who had purchased a glass house on a short sale two years ago. He owned a string of furniture discount shops that sold a low line of couches, chairs and bedroom items that no one in Centerport would have been caught dead bringing into their house. Mrs. Swenson, who Jack realized was not the eye candy that Swenson had on his arm, had had so much plastic surgery than even his children didn't recognize her the last time she came off the operating table. People in Centerport saw little of her as she was a dedicated amateur lepidopterist who roamed the world in search of rare butterflies.

Jack decided to exercise his privilege as the owner of the dealership and opt for a closer look at the marvelous specimen of womanhood that Swenson had brought in. He would not have been surprised to see staple holes in her mid-section, which he was delighted to find available for viewing. This was indeed a one-trick pony.

"I'm Jack Poor, *the* Jack Poor," he said, holding out his hand to Alfie. "Welcome to my dealership."

"My name is Alfie Swenson."

"I know who you are," Jack said absently as he turned to give his attention to Florence leaving Swenson staring at the back of Jack's suit coat.

"We'd like that silver car, there," she said, pointing to the Verite 300. "I just love it. It's really me. Don't you think so, Alfie?"

Alfie might have thought so, but his expression was not unlike that of a man suffering an attack of acid reflux. Looking around, he could see one salesman after another seeming to find a pressing reason to come onto the floor and busy himself near the Verite. He obviously did not appreciate having Florence the object of these gawkers. His annoyance showed when he barked, "Look, if you're going to let me buy this car, say so. If not, we'll take a walk."

Jack put his arm on Alfie's shoulder and turned on the charm. After all, while enjoying the landscape of a delectable woman was nectar for the imagination, a man with a checkbook was manna for the bottom line. "Mr. Swenson, may I call you Alfie?" he asked than then not waiting for a reply said, "I assure you that we're here to sell cars and from where I stand, this car has your name written all over it. We're having a hell of a time keeping these in stock. I hate to give up a display car." There were several more like it outside, but Jack was sure Alfie hadn't noticed. "But, we're here to serve our customers. If this is the car you want, it's yours."

"Then, do it. How long is this going to take?"

Nothing like a man in heat looking to buy a car, Jack thought. *His brain is in his pants and my hand is in his wallet. He won't know what the hell he's buying. One nice payday on the way.*

"Well, Mr. Swenson, I'm sure Mr. Swenson here can have the papers ready for you to sign in just a few minutes. Are you interested in looking at our finance package? We've got some very attractive rates."

"You take credit cards, right?" Alfie asked.

"Of course," Jack replied. "Credit cards are as good as cash." He smiled. And he might have added, but did not, better than a check which would have to be certified and leave little room for Spud to load the deal with extras.

"I'd like to try it on," Florence giggled, approaching the Verite's passenger side door.

If ever a woman had the ability to make getting into a car look X-rated, she was that woman. One of the salesmen quickly stepped up to the car to open the door for her. But instead of opening it and stepping back toward the rear of the car, he stood in front of the door, pulling it to him and stepping backward toward the front of the car. Still holding the door, he positioned himself so that he had an unobstructed view of the car seat. As Florence sat down, she swung first one leg and then the other inside which, for an extended moment, caused her short dress to open, giving the salesman a clear view all the way up her thighs to the frilly white triangle that passed for her underwear. It was an old salesman's trick called a "beaver shoot," and the salesmen at Jack Poor Motors were all expert marksmen when it came to beavers.

Spud pulled Jack aside and said, "Defiantly a spot delivery." *(Translation: The customer buys and takes delivery of the car on the spot.)*

"This guy is so hot to get in her pants, he's gonna pay any price we give him," Jack Poor said. "Bang him for a full sticker. No discount. Then bump him with every goddamn thing we can add to the invoice. An extended warranty, rust protection, fabric protection, paint protection, the whole nine yards."

Spud invited Alfie and Florence to sit down at his desk. Jack Poor, who normally would have excused himself and let his salesman conclude the deal, found it convenient to take up a position that afforded a view down Florence's front.

It was not often that a lay down *(Translation: A customer ready to pay the full sticker price without asking for a discount or bothering to negotiate the price.)* walked into the showroom. Especially Jack Poor's showroom. Spud maintained a steady stream of obsequious what-a-great-deal-I'm-giving-you-because-I-really-like-you persiflage, all the while adding up the numbers and tacking on every option and warranty coverage he could think of. Spud Kapock could have been talking to stone.

"Whatever, whatever! Let's get this done," Alfie kept saying. "Here's my credit card. Where do I sign?"

As Spud hurried to fill out the order, Florence popped up and circled the car, caressing it in the most suggestive manner. When Florence returned to Alfie's side, she purred, "I get to drive it a lot, right?"

"Anytime you want. In fact, you can take it home every night, if you like."

"What will the others in the store say?"

"It's my car. I'm the boss. So it's none of their damn business."

"Ooooh, Alfie," she purred. "You're the best boss I've ever had." She supplemented her appreciation by casually rubbing her right breast on his arm and whispering in his ear what appeared, to the onlookers, as a salacious secret. Alfie's carnal reward was fully primed.

"I can drive it off the floor, right? I mean, like right now?" Alfie's impatience was bordering on the comical.

"Right," Spud replied, doing his best not to laugh at the scene being played out across his desk.

"What do I do about license plates?"

"We can put our dealer plates on until you get it registered."

"Good. Do it."

"George!" Spud called to one of the salesmen. "Put dealer plates on this Verite."

Alfie signed the credit card chit without even looking at the total. It could have been for double the amount, but at that moment, he didn't appear to care. Once the plates were on, Swenson and Florence got into the car.

"Would you like me to explain the controls and some of the features?" Swenson asked.

"Some other time."

"If you drive it around back, we'll fill it up with gas."

"I'll get it later."

Two salesmen pushed back the large sliding glass doors that were installed so that display cars could be easily driven on and off the showroom floor. Alfie started the sport coupe and drove it through the open doors, down the driveway and into the street. The entire transaction had been completed in twenty-three minutes. A record for Jack Poor Motors. The salesmen who had been witness to the transaction were useless, at least more useless than normal, for the next three hours as they entertained each other with their individual recounting and imitations of what they had witnessed.

The Verite 300 left Greenwich on I-95, took the ramp to I-287, and headed toward Tarrytown, New York, on the Hudson River. When Alfie got to Tarrytown, he left 287, and took Route 9 north along the Hudson River. Destination? Two days of *coitus noninterruptus* at the plush Hudson Resort and Spa lay ahead. The road was lightly traveled and the swelling in his trousers seemed to have a correlating effect on the pressure he was putting on the gas pedal. He never saw the cop with the radar sitting off to the side. The road began to wind and Swenson, who envisioned himself as an unrequited Mario Andretti, decided to impress Florence with his driving skills.

The road felt good. The car felt good. Suddenly he felt her unzip his fly. The blond head descended slowly into his lap. The road signs indicated a curve ahead and announced that 25mph was the appropriate speed. The Verite 300 was doing at least sixty.

It was after five o'clock when Jack Poor walked out of his dealership. He was about to get in his car when a flatbed trailer pulled into the dealership carrying a Verite 300 that looked as if it had been run over by a truck.

"What's this?" Jack asked the driver.

"This, I think," the driver nodded in the direction of the Verite, "is one sorry looking hunk of metal. We didn't know what to do with it. Cops said since the car had your dealer plates on it, we should bring it here."

Jack immediately recognized it as the car Alfie Swenson and Florence had driven off the floor not six hours before. "Where's the owner? And the bimbo? When he left here, he was with one great looking piece of tail."

"And he still is. They're both on a slab in a morgue somewhere."

"They're dead?" he asked, genuinely shocked.

The driver shrugged and nodded.

"Jesus! How'd it happen?"

"It was pretty much self-inflicted. According to the cops, they were chasing this guy up Route 9 north of Tarrytown. He had this car flyin.' Fifty-five, sixty maybe. And considering they found him with his Johnson hangin' out and her head in his lap, he was flyin' in more ways than one. What got 'em was the sucker curve."

"Sucker curve?" Jack asked.

"Yeah. That's what they call a descending radius curve."

"Which is …?"

"A curve that tends to turn in on itself. At high speeds it can be tricky to negotiate. 'Specially if you got some broad's mouth on your dick. The cop chasin' 'em said it looked like the rear end spun out and then

WHAP! The car wrapped itself around a big fucking oak tree. Considering his mind was in his lap, he probably never knew what hit him. I'm sure it won't be a big surprise to learn she wasn't the woman in the car. They tracked Mrs. Swenson down using the address on his driver's license. The maid told us she's off traveling somewhere. Here you wanna see a copy of the police report?" Jack nodded and the driver handed it to him. "Keep it. I don't want it."

Jack shook his head as he read the report, "Can you imagine what she's going to say when she reads this and finds out Swenson died while getting a BJ?"

"Don't think they'll ever give it to her."

"Yeah?"

"One of the cops told me they were going to omit that detail from their final report. They said there was no need to make things worse for the wife. Her husband's dead. He was with another woman. That's painful enough. The full truth of what happened sure as hell isn't going to make her feel any better. Y'know what I mean?"

Jack nodded to indicate that he did know what the flatbed driver meant, then told him where to put the wreck. He shook his head slowly as he thought about how lucky he'd been that Swenson had put the car on his credit card.

"Damn," he said aloud to no one but himself, "if Swenson had opted for the finance package, I'd be holdin' the bag right now. It would have taken me months to get paid."

Patton Once Removed

Petula Poor had not expected Fletcher to accompany Cosima and the girls to Centerport for the surprise birthday party she was giving her father, Bumper McCoy, the patriarch of the family. She greeted his arrival with about the same level of enthusiasm that she would have welcomed a meter reader from the electric company. Like the meter reader, Fletcher had come unannounced, had little to do, wasn't expected to stay long, and Petula would barely notice when he left.

Jack Poor arrived home at about six, just an hour before Bumper McCoy's surprise party was scheduled to begin. His attire immediately brought a disapproving grimace from Petula. His powder blue sport coat and light yellow slacks might be acceptable in the dealership, but not at Bumper's party. "We are going to change our clothes, aren't we." It wasn't a question; it was a demand. "Your grey suit has been laid out on the bed." Jack nodded, said nothing, and obeyed.

While Fletcher had done his best to avoid more than twice-a-year visits to Petula and Jack, he was always amazed to find that the master of Jack Poor Motors was, in his own home, more like a boarder who had come to live under Petula's roof and was expected to appear only at meals. Generally, Jack found refuge in his den, watching television and reading the car ads from his competitors.

By six-thirty the guests started to arrive so that they could be in place by seven to surprise Bumper. Fletcher wondered just how much of a surprise it would be considering the driveway was full of high-end cars. Jack and Fletcher were assigned by Petula to stand by the front door like doorstops. They greeted the guests who had little inclination to offer more than a "hello" or "where's the bathroom" and then move on to the foyer to mix with more socially appropriate company. At the appointed hour, Bumper's chauffeur found that he could not get past all the guest's cars, which meant the old man had to walk halfway up the long drive, past all the cars in order to be surprised. Well, if not surprised, he was certainly pleased to be serenaded with a chorus of Happy Birthday, Bumper.

class=WordSection3>

Bumper made the rounds of the guests, greeting them by name and thanking them for helping celebrate his seventy-fifth birthday. He proudly proclaimed, to one and all that, for reasons unknown, it was only fitting his birthday was on June 21st, the summer solstice. Jack and Fletcher were last to receive his attention.

Bumper looked at the two men as if he had just happened upon two party crashers. He jumped right over the more conventional greetings like "Hello. How are you?" and leveled a verbal karate chop. "You two still haven't figured it out, have you?" Without losing a beat he continued, "The car business is for losers. Wall Street. That's where the smart people and smart money live. It's obvious where you two live. Or I should say, 'don't live.' Hell, if you tried to move where the smart money lives, they'd probably burn your house down."

He broke into paroxysms of laugher. "Haw, haw, hen, haw, hee, ho, hack, hack awhoop, awhoop, hack, arggggb, swapshssss!" He bent over, phlegm shooting from his mouth. He sounded as if he might choke and die. Petula heard the hacking, ran to his side, and started slapping him hard on the back.

"A little harder," Jack said in an aside to Fletcher, "and she might kill the old bastard. Wouldn't that break your heart?" He bit down hard on a short laugh.

After a few moments Bumper recovered. The butler appeared and announced to all that dinner was to be served.

As soon as dinner was over, Fletcher and Jack slipped outside. The front courtyard was filled with Benzes and Bentleys and Rolls and a Ferrari or two.

"Looks like a used car lot for the financially handicapped." Jack lit a cigar. "Can you believe it; not one of my cars among them?" His tone was ripe with sarcasm. "Want a cigar?"

"No thanks, I'll pass."

"Have you ever seen so many phony fuckers in one place in your life? Most of them hate Bumper. It's like they're afraid if they don't kiss his behind, they'll be excommunicated from the country club."

"They did seem to grovel a bit."

"Unctuous bastards." He took a long draw on his cigar and then turned to Fletcher and said, "Did you know we're having a Sell-A-Thon tomorrow?"

Fletcher shook his head.

Slowly, the master of Jack Poor Motors was reemerging. "It's our biggest tent sale of the year. This will be a hell of an opportunity for you to see how we move the iron. Your guys in Detroit could learn a thing or two about what it takes to sell cars, if they spent a couple days with me. This business that you guys preach in your training programs of suckin' up to customers is bullshit. Maybe those assholes at Mercedes and BMW can kiss the customer's ass and get 'em to buy cars, but not us. At our end of the market, we have to nail the weasels to the floor and squeeze 'em. That's what works for us." Jack took another long drag on his cigar. "You want to stay here tomorrow or come down to the dealership with me and learn how to sell cars?"

Now there's a Hobson's choice, if there ever was one, Fletcher thought. I can spend the day being insulted by a mother-in-law who hates me or I can sit in a dealership and listen to my obnoxious father-in-law pontificate about the art of selling cars to weasels. Fletcher elected to take a pass on both options and booked himself on the six a.m. flight back to Detroit.

II

Jack arrived at the dealership early to get ready for the Saturday morning sales meeting. Jack loved sales meetings. Other than selling a car for full sticker, there was little he enjoyed more than to get up in front of his fifteen salesmen and set the tone for the day by motivating them to achieve even higher levels of sales.

Jack slapped his sales manager, Spud Kapock on the back as they walked toward the training room. "I'm really pumped this morning. We're taking no prisoners today."

The man on his way to the sales meeting was no longer Jack Poor, car dealer. He had transformed himself into an automotive General Patton, ready to lead his boys into battle. Jack looked like a man who could smell the action. Taste the blood.

"By the time we close our doors today, the sales floor is going to be running green … green with money," he said confidently. "Everyone here?" Jack asked Spud as they stepped inside the room.

"Looks like it." Spud said looking around the room. "Oh, Owens called in sick so he won't be here."

"Bullshit. He's hung over. Fire the bastard."

"Done," Spud said.

The training room was about twenty by forty with chairs lined up schoolroom style facing a large American flag and a white marking board. Webb found it interesting that Jack purposely avoided eye contact as he walked toward the front. Clearly part of the show.

Jack slowly turned to his salesmen, all of whom were dressed in coats and ties. A quick glance around the room told Jack that his troops were, variously, half asleep, bored, scared, detached, interested in whatever they were reading in the newspaper, or finishing the last of the coffee and Dunkin' Donuts that was always brought in for these meetings.

"Okay," Jack said, "let's get started. For any of you that are too hung over to have noticed, this is Saturday, June 22nd.It's a *Jack Poor Sell-A-Thon* day. *You* are going to make money today. *I* am going to make money today. We are *all* going to make money today!"

With that, he opened his briefcase and held up the fifteen-hundred-dollar wad of bills. "Listen up. Here's the skinny: I'm paying $100 to each of the first three guys who close deals this morning. I got $200 for the best gross. I am giving $400 to the guy who sells the most cars today. And there's $200 for the guy who can get rid of that '97 Blue Dodge that's been sitting on the lot for the last four months."

Jack unfolded a newspaper and held up the full-page ad that had appeared in several local papers. "In our Sell-A-Thon ad, you will notice that we feature the Red Verite that's sitting out under the tent for '$1.00 Over Invoice.' Be aware that we are not, I repeat, we are not selling any other Verite for $1 over invoice, just that one. Got that? Just *that* one. Now, listen carefully: There's a reward for any guy who sells that car. And the reward is …" Jack paused for effect and looked at every man in the room, "… the reward is *you lose your fuckin' job.* Your ass is outta here! Let me repeat that for the benefit of you rookies: That Red Verite under the tent does *not* leave this lot. Your job is to convince people that they *do not want* that Red Verite. You'll say or do whatever it takes *not* to sell that car. I don't care if you have to pry their fingers off the door and drag 'em away. That car stays right where it is. You will sell them *off* that car and *onto* one with a full markup or I will personally come out on the lot, rip off your head, and shit down your neck!"

Jack was loving himself. He was in overdrive and cruising until one of the rookies raised his hand. "But that doesn't sound very ethical, Mr. Poor," the rookie said with concern. "How can you offer something in the paper and then not deliver?"

"What the fuck does ethics have to do with it?" Jack spit back. "You're not here to feel sorry for these weasels. You're here to put their asses in a car and to clean out their wallets."

Jack took a breath and looked around the room. "How many of you live in Centerport?"

No one raised his hand.

"Exactly. Not one of you. You can't afford to. But, the people who walk in here today *can* afford to live in Centerport, which means they have money and that makes them the enemy. If they can screw us out of making a profit on one of our cars, you can bet your sweet bippy that they will. Well, they can't screw Jack Poor because I screw 'em first. Read my lips: These people are not your friends. They are people with money. But when they walk in here, it's no longer their money. It's my money and I want it. Your job is to get my money, *your* money, out of their pockets and onto Spud's desk. I don't care if you have to squeeze 'em, bump 'em, bush 'em, or whack 'em; your job is to get every last nickel out of their pockets."

Jack paused to catch his breath. He had worked up a significant sweat. Then, without thinking, he began to mop his forehead with the eraser from the white marking board.

"One more thing, and this is for the benefit of you rookies: Nobody, and I mean *nobody,* walks. *(Translation: A customer leaves the showroom without buying a car.)* If you can't close 'em, you pull the alarm and turn 'em over … T.O. 'em, to Spud here. You rookies can learn something from Spud. When he puts a customer in the hot box, they don't come out until they've lost ten pounds and signed on the dotted line. Then, when they come to pick up the car, he bangs 'em for a few more bucks just for having been such an asshole and given us a hard time. I love it when he does that. If I could only clone him." Jack looked admiringly at his sales manager who was basking in the adulation. "Any questions?"

No one raised a hand. The rookies looked shell-shocked. The veterans shrugged with a same old, same old expression.

Jack clearly did not expect any questions. He clapped his hands and shouted, "Okay, troops, let's get out there on the floor and ... MAKE ... ME ... SOME ... MONEY!"

For a moment, Jack expected, but was clearly disappointed not to hear, a rousing "let's go get 'em" response, like a gung-ho football team leaving the locker room or the dough boys going over the top. Instead, he saw three incredulous, dismayed rookies and a dozen veterans wearing vague, ambivalent expressions shuffle out of the room like a bunch of people with no particular place to go and in no hurry to get there.

Mrs. Swenson Pays a Visit

Just after twelve, the screaming began. Mrs. Delia Swenson, a seriously overweight, middle-aged women with flaming red hair, dressed in what looked like sweat clothes, had commandeered a place in the middle of Tom Poor's showroom. She started screaming, "Jack Poor killed my husband! He sells cars that kill people! Jack Poor should be arrested and sent to the electric chair for what he did. He's a killer! A mother-fucking killer!"

If her objective was to attract attention, she certainly achieved that in short order. She looked like the kind of wild-eyed, bent-on-revenge woman that would, at any minute, produce a machine gun out of her sweat pants and start shooting up the place. Customers who had just walked into the dealership did an immediate one-eighty and fled. Others cowered behind their salesmen, most of whom were also looking for cover.

Spud Kapock stood up, and looked around to see if anyone was going to deal with the woman. It appeared that all the salesmen had suddenly found someplace else to be.

"Are you Jack Poor?" She screamed as Spud approached. "Are you the miserable bastard that sold my husband that deathtrap on wheels?"

"No, I'm not Mr. Poor. I'm sure he'd be more than happy to talk with you. But first, you've got to calm down and control yourself."

"Control myself? You mean like my husband couldn't control your fucking car?"

Spud reached out to lay a reassuring hand on her shoulder, "Please believe me, Mr. Poor was truly saddened to hear of your loss."

"Lay a hand on her, and I'll sue your ass for sexual molestation and assault and battery." The voice belonged to a squat, little clone of Danny DeVito.

"Who are you?" Spud asked.

The clone reached into his pocket and handed Spud a card that identified him as Abner Slipwalker, Personal Injury Lawyer. "I'm Mrs. Swenson's lawyer. Any attempt to remove my client from these premises will be documented." With that said, he pulled out is iPhone held it up, preparing to record any attempt to remove the hysterical Mrs. Swenson.

"Wait here," Spud said, "and please try to calm your client. I'll find Jack Poor." He left Mrs. Swenson and Slipwalker and ran up the stairs that led to Jack's office.

Jack met him at the door. "What the hell is going on down there? What's all that screaming?"

"Swenson's wife is here and she wants to see you. She's hysterical. She's screaming that you killed her husband."

"What?" Jack was incredulous. "Get her the fuck off the floor before she scares away all my customers."

"Should I bring her up here?

"Does she look like she might have a gun?"

"A gun?" Spud asked.

"You can't be too careful these days. If you're sure she hasn't got a gun, bring her up."

Spud returned to the floor and asked Slipwalker and Mrs. Swenson to follow him back upstairs. Mrs. Swenson remained reasonably restrained until she entered Jack's office. Once inside, she let fly again.

"You killed my husband! You knew that car was a deathtrap! You're going to pay for this! I'll have you in court. I'll take you all the way to the Supreme Court, if I have to. I'll see you in the electric chair!" She had gone over the edge, a fact not lost on her lawyer, who decided that he'd better step in before Mrs. Swenson started breaking things.

"Delia, Delia," he said stepping in front of her. "I think you should sit down and let me handle things from here." He looked at Jack, "As you can see, she's very distraught over this."

"I can see that," Jack said with matter-of-fact frankness.

"Mr. Poor, my name is Abner Slipwalker, and I represent Mrs. Swenson. We plan to bring suit against your dealership, you and, of course, the manufacturer, for the death of Adolph Swenson and his...his....

"Secretary," Mrs. Swenson volunteered.

. "Slipwalker pointed toward the couch adjacent to Jack's desk, "May we sit down?"

"Be my guest," Jack said in his most accommodating tone.

Slipwalker and Mrs. Swenson settled onto Jack's couch.

"Excuse me for asking, but isn't this a little unusual for you and your client to announce in person that you're going to sue me? I don't want to tell you how to do your job, Mr. Slipwalker, but I don't believe this is the way these things are supposed to work."

Mrs. Swenson interrupted, "I have to go to the bathroom. Bad."

Jack pointed to a door on the other side of the room. "That's my private washroom. Please feel free."

Spud couldn't get over Jack's measured and calm demeanor. It was not like him. By now, he'd fully expected him to toss both Slipwalker and Mrs. Swenson out of his office.

As soon as Mrs. Swenson closed the door, Slipwalker stood up and took a seat next to Jack's desk. "Understand, this was not my idea. In fact, I advised strongly against it. But this is the one-month anniversary of Mr. Swenson's death, and she insisted on visiting the scene of the crime."

"Excuse me?" Jack retorted incredulously. "Scene of the crime? If my memory serves me correctly, the *accident* happened over in Westchester."

"True, but the car came from here and, well ..." he shrugged, "she's been under a lot of strain since the funeral." He turned and checked to be sure that bathroom door was still closed. "I had no idea she would react the way she did. But you have to understand, her husband's death has been a terrible blow."

Jack got up from behind his desk and stared at the little man for a moment, then picked up a chair and set it down very close to Slipwalker. Godfather close, which is to say, uncomfortably close. "Abner, may I call you Abner?" he began

Abner nodded.

"Abner, based on your performance so far today, I'd say as a personal injury lawyer, you'd make a great lamp shade. Let me give you a bit of free advice; if you're going to sue someone, you don't pay them a social visit first."

"I told you, my client insisted on coming."

"And you let her?"

"I had no choice. If I had refused, she would have come without me."

"I'm not a lawyer, Abner, but if I were, I certainly would not have let her put on that performance in my showroom."

"She ran inside before I could stop her. She is very determined."

"She is also nuts."

"I would prefer distraught to nuts. I don't think you'll be able to defend yourself, based on her emotional state of mind. Her case is truly tragic. And you and your company are going to have to answer some very serious questions."

Jack remained exceedingly calm and controlled.

"You're new at this, aren't you Abner?"

"New? New at what?"

"PI. Personal injury law. I mean, you don't strike me as having had much experience in matters like this."

"If you think you're going to put me off with insults …"

Jack cut him off. "My apologies. I am sorry." He said it with such sincerity that it sounded as though he might even mean it. "Far be it from me to insult you or your client. Here at Jack Poor Motors, everyone who walks in the front door is entitled to our utmost respect. I insist on it. Even personal injury lawyers. In fact, especially, PI lawyers." Jack leaned even closer to Slipwalker, laying a paternal hand on the little man's shoulder. "Let me make sure I understand your intentions. Mrs. Swenson feels we were responsible for her husband's death, and she's considering a lawsuit."

Slipwalker nodded slightly, growing increasingly uncomfortable at his close proximity to Jack.

"That's your right. Far be it from me to suggest you not exercise your rights. I invite you to sue. In fact, I would like you to file very soon so that this matter can be settled in court and not on our showroom floor. When can I expect you to file?"

Slipwalker was taken aback. He had never had a potential defendant invite a lawsuit. "What are you up to, Poor?" Slipwalker rose from his chair and moved to the center of the room.

The sound of the toilet flushing arrived as Mrs. Swenson opened the door to the toilet. "I think you better get a plunger. It's stopped up."

"Thank you for letting me know," Jack said most graciously.

Slipwalker put on his best PI face and tried to regain the initiative. "I don't know what kind of game you're playing, Poor, but this Mr. Nice-Nice act of yours is not going to put us off. We are going to sue."

"You're damn right," Mrs. Swenson volunteered.

"If you feel you have a case, I invite you to do just that." Jack stood up, walked to his desk and fished for a business card from the middle drawer. "This is my lawyer," he said handing Slipwalker the card. "Now, I ask you again, when may we expect you to file?"

Slipwalker was clearly nonplussed. "We'll be filing in the next couple weeks, you can count on it," he said, clearly determined to show this car dealer that he could not be put off with whateverthehell he was trying to do.

"Fine," Jack answered pleasantly. "I look forward to it." Jack smiled like a chess player who has just called checkmate after three moves. Oh, I almost forgot, maybe you'd like to read the original police report about the accident.

Sliipwaker took the report and scanned it quickly He looked like an actor who had forgotten his lines. He did not know what to say." He turned to Mrs. Swenson and took her arm. "We need to go, now." He took Mrs. Swenson's arm and pulled her toward the door.

She pulled away from his grasp. "What? Wait a minute! Let go of me! When do I get my money from this sonofabitch? You said he'd want to offer a settlement to get us off his back."

"Let's talk in the car."

"Wait. Give me that report," she said snatching it from his hand. It took less than a minute for her to get to the salient information. "That son-of-a bitch. He said the only reason she hired that whore was because she had some unique skills. Now I know what he meant. by unique skills." She tossed the report back at Slipwalker who was still attempting to pull her toward the door. "I'm going to kill that bastard and while I'm at it I'm going to kill her too," she screamed.

Slipwalker opened the door and began to force her out.

Jack Poor, appearing calm and unruffled, stood up and in a most gracious and appreciative tone said." Mrs. Swenson, I want tot hank you for telling me about the toilet. Have a good day. Oh, and thanks to your late husband for shopping Jack Poor Motors." Then the salesman that he was, he said, "By the way, if you're interested, I can make you a hellava deal today on the Green Verita."

The Man in the Mud Brown Suit

The first time Charlie Fair likened himself to Louis XV, his wife presumed he was kidding. Every time after that, she was not so sure. On occasion, Olivia would find Charlie in front of his mirror, admiring himself and saying, "Je sui le roi. Le roi pouvoir non faux. *(Translation: I am the king. The king can do no wrong.)* He had no idea if the French grammar was correct and frankly didn't care. It was the intent that mattered. One of Henry Ford's wives reported that Henry said exactly the same thing–but, in English. Charlie felt that he showed a lot more class by saying it in French. While the house he lived in was not Versailles, it wasn't your typical center hall colonial either. Not with twenty-eight rooms, a guesthouse, a pool house, and an attached five-car garage with servants' quarters.

Charlie surrounded himself with things French, ranging from period *bureau placs* and commodes, *Limoges* porcelains, classical and neo-impressionist paintings, to his butler, who hailed from Maubeuge, and two tempting French truffles from Marseilles. He also imported two gardeners to maintain the grounds. To save money, he recruited them from Quebec. Though they were not French, they sounded like they were to everyone but the butler and the Marseilles truffles, who claimed that whatever it was they spoke, it certainly wasn't *their* French. While Charlie's backyard was a mere fraction the size of Louis' at Versailles, it did have fountains, garden pools, many flower beds, and crushed white gravel walks.

In fair weather, Charlie, like Louis, would invite his guests to promenade with him through the gardens. And, like Louis, those who strolled with him took note of who Charlie chose to have walk with him. If you were asked to walk along side Charlie, you were considered to be "in." If you were assigned to follow behind, you were on shaky ground. And if you weren't there at all, it meant you were either temporarily out of favor or in line to be axed.

Charlie looked forward to any and every opportunity to hold court at his home. He found a perverse delight in demonstrating his ability to bring a smile to the face of a manager one minute and then shoot an arrow of fear into his heart the next. He also class=WordSection4>

enjoyed confounding his guests with obtuse, cryptic remarks that defied concise interpretation, but intimated that he was in the process of reevaluating, and adding to, the list of those who would feel the ax. In his mind he may have been Louis XV, but to many of his managers, he was Robespierre.

It was such fun to be the king, surrounded with endless opulence and obsequious supplicants, all in the comfort of his very own Versailles. Yet for all the pleasure Charlie took from the house, it was a house he would never have shown to his stockholders. It was a house that spoke of a man who had made a great deal of money, a man who had earned the title, Captain of Industry, a man who had the genius to make his stockholders rich. What the house did not speak to, did not even hint at, was that it was the home of a man whose company ranked dead last in the American car market A man whose company stock price hovered regularly just above having itself delisted on the New York Stock Exchange. In fact, it was the house of neither man, but of Charlie's wife, Olivia Byrd Fair. She had inherited it from her maternal grandmother, a Chrysler married to a Vanderbilt. Grandfather Vanderbilt had wandered west for a time in 1903 and built what he regarded as a summer retreat on the shores of Lake St. Clair. Along with the house, Olivia was the recipient of a trust that was well nigh bottomless. She was truly of old money.

The brunch for her petition committee was, of course, Olivia's idea. Her original guest list had numbered no more than thirty. But Charlie felt that no affair at his house–other than a selective dinner–should number less than one hundred. So he expanded the guest list with invitations of his own. When he informed Olivia to expect about seventy more than she'd planned, she was angry. She became furious when she looked over the additional names and found at least three women who, rumor had it, claimed a recent history with Charlie. Did he think he could hide them from her? Did he think she wouldn't notice? Again, as so many times in the past, she knew she would be the subject of Grosse Pointe gossip: "How can she not know?" "Did you see who Charlie was talking to?" "I can't believe Olivia would allow him to invite *her*." "The story I heard was …" and so the tittle-tattle would go. It was not limited to just the women. The men took even greater delight in speculating on

Charlie's conquests until, on one occasion, two men found themselves confronted with the embarrassing fact that they were talking about their own wives.

While the gossip was always titillating at the Fair's parties, no one ever understood how Olivia could rise above the humiliation engendered by Charlie's reputation. She resolved never to emulate Ann McDowell Ford and create a scene by hauling her husband off a dance floor when her husband's dance partner became overly aggressive. Olivia Fair was far too proud, too dignified for that. If she suffered, and the assumption was that she did, she did so in private. She was liked and respected by her friends, but pitied as well. If she had been aware of their pity, it might have crushed her.

Yes, Olivia thought as she finished dressing, *I will endure this as always. And if the vodka helps ease the pain, well ...?*

II

Muffy and Preston Waddington were greeted at the front door by the Fair's butler from Maubeuge, who directed then into the enormous living room. "Cozy" was not a word that Waddington would have used to describe the room in which he stood. *You could play basketball in here,* he thought, although it was hard to image someone dribbling through the ornate furnishings and driving for a backboard nailed over the great marble fireplace. It was even larger than Muffy's Grandfather's house in Greenwich, which, by comparison, was a mere handball court.

The walls were covered in red damask, which served as a background for so many paintings that Waddington expected, at any minute, to see a museum guide leading an art class on a tour. The ceiling had been faux painted to give the impression of looking through a large oval opening into a blue sky where puffy, white clouds provided perches for naked cherubs. Waddington decided that the artist had displayed his sense of bourgeois resentment in the facial expressions he painted on the cherubs. Each peered down from the ceiling, appearing dismayed and disgusted by the bejeweled women and grey-suited clones who ravenously accosted waiters carrying trays of hors-d'oeuvres, stuffing their faces between hugs and handshakes as they vied for recognition and favor from the King.

As Waddington surveyed the guests, he immediately began to suspect that every man, other than himself, had been privy to a pre-party notification that the uniform-of-the-day was a dark-gray suit, white shirt, and conservative tie. Waddington had presumed that a Sunday afternoon party the first of June might find the guests in more summer-like attire. So he opted for an electric blue shirt, bright-yellow tie, and his mud-brown suit. He had ignored, or possibly forgotten, that the suit always wrinkled badly, creating the impression that he'd slept in it. One thing was for certain– there was no way Muffy would lose him in the crowd. For a moment, he thought about going home and changing, but Livonia would have been a two-hour round trip, and the party would have been over by the time he got back.

Waddington took cover behind Muffy, who was wearing a lavender Mary McFadden frock with big puffs and poufs on her shoulders and waist that made her look twice her size. It was a curious choice on Muffy's part, as the outfit tended to obscure her hours on the Butt Buster. He decided that she must be making a fashion statement. From his wifely redoubt, he scanned the room and recognized Popper and three other men from the executive floors, all of whom were titled with VP or higher. The rest of the guests were unknown to him.

Olivia Fair pirouetted her way through the milling bodies and greeted Muffy as a true sister of the cause. The cause, of course, being the effort to block the building of low-income housing in Grosse Pointe. The women exchanged compliments on each other's dress, hair style, what have you, and then Muffy stepped aside to reveal the man in the mud-brown suit, looking as if he were attempting to emulate Harry Houdini and vanish.

"Olivia, this is my husband." She said it with the same enthusiasm that she might have said, "This is my pet goldfish."

Olivia was working the crowd with her left hand, the right appearing glued to a tumbler of what Waddington presumed was vodka. Water did not seem to be a likely alternative since she seemed to list slightly to the left when she spoke. She looked at Waddington's mud-brown suit, then turned to Muffy and gushed her approval, "Oh, your husband is an iconoclast. I just adore a man who isn't afraid to stand out in a crowd. It says so much about his sense of self."

With that she held up her left hand to Waddington upon which rested something that looked like the Hope

Diamond. "I'm Olivia Fair, so delightful to have you here."

Waddington looked at the proffered hand and wasn't sure whether protocol at this level of society called for him to shake it or kiss it. He took the ends of her fingers and wiggled them in a ridiculous fashion, then retreated to a position behind the puff on Muffy's right shoulder. From that vantage point, he had a chance to assess Mrs. Fair. He found himself quite taken with her appearance. She was not at all what he'd expected, but then, he wasn't exactly sure what he had expected. He guessed her to be in her mid-to-late forties. She was small, with a well-defined figure that had certainly held the years at bay. A little liposuction maybe? A face-lift? Maybe. Maybe not. It made no difference. Her black, shoulder-length hair was so perfectly coiffed that, for a moment, he thought it might be a wig. It wasn't. But it was her face that fascinated him. What was it about her face that he found so mesmerizing?

"Waddington!" Charlie's loud greeting cut through the rising din of the vapid cocktail party conversations. "Olivia, have you met Pres Waddington?"

"I just did," she responded.

"Pres has just created the best advertising concept we've ever had."

Olivia looked at Waddington, "Are you in advertising?

He never had a chance to answer.

"No, that's what's so amazing. Pres is our sales training manager and editor of the *Company Eyes Only* report. But he probably should be in advertising. A truly multitalented man. Great asset to the company."

Having favored Waddington with his praise, Charlie made it clear that he did not intend to linger long. He had barely said "… to the company," when his eyes began darting about the room in search of something or someone of more immediate interest. Finding it or her or them, he immediately excused himself. "Catch you later."

"Well," Olivia said, "I must say, you seem to have impressed my husband. It's not like him to go on like that about his employees. Are you as talented as he suggests?"

It was a leading question, but before Waddington could suggest that Charlie had been a bit overly generous with his praise, Muffy and Olivia were swept up and carried off by several women whose faces had that I-must-tell-you-about-this-now look of urgency that women at cocktail parties often have.

As he stood alone in the crowd, enduring the occasional stares of guests who seemed to be wondering why the man in the mud-brown suit was out of uniform, he felt very much like a Toyota in the Cadillac parking lot. No one ever dared park a Japanese import in front of a GM facility, just as, apparently, no one ever came to a Fair party in a mud-brown suit.

Waddington could not help but notice that Muffy, on the other hand, literally glowed with delight. She was like someone who, after many years away, had returned to familiar and comfortable surroundings. For her, the Fair's house and Grosse Pointe must have seemed like a small corner of Greenwich transported to the hinterlands. Waddington watched as she infiltrated a group of women who all looked as if they had picked their way through display trays at Tiffany's and were currently in some type of competition to see who could drape, pin, stick, or in some manner affix the largest amount of plunder on their fingers, necks, ears, and clothing.

Marooned as he was in the middle of the room, he tried to appear absorbed in admiring the art on the walls. In fact, he was looking for a refuge. On the other side of the room, across from the entrance to the foyer, he saw what appeared to be a forest of Ficus trees, at least a dozen. A man could wander behind those and disappear, he decided. He had barely taken a step in that direction when a voice said, "I don't know if you're aware of it, Pres, but your pants don't match your suit coat."

Reflexively, Waddington looked at his pants. *My God, he's right.* He had accidentally put on a pair of brown slacks, almost the same color and material as his suit pants, but not quite. Then, in an attempt to mount a face-saving defense, he said. "The light bulb in my closet was burned out." He looked up to see who had nothing better to do than comment on his wardrobe. *Oh my God! Perkins Byrd.*

Perkins looked him up and down and smiled. "Well, Waddington, it looks like you didn't get the memo on the uniform of the day."

Waddington did his best to hide his embarrassment behind a short laugh. "I guess there's always one guy who doesn't get the message."

"Your wife involved with Olivia, is she?"

Waddington nodded, "She's on the petition committee."

"Good for her," Perkins said. He leaned close to Waddington and said, "Charlie tells me your father-in-law hasn't heard anything from the woman's lawyer."

"Nothing. I talked to him again yesterday and he said he doesn't expect to hear from her. He contends it was totally the driver's fault, and the police records will back him up. Or as my father-in-law so eloquently put it, 'It's all bullshit.'"

Perkins was thoughtful for a moment and then said, "Well, let's hope so. But for some reason, I have a bad feeling about this." For a moment he lapsed into some private thought, then snapped back and clapped Waddington on the shoulder as he glanced around the room. "I guess I better go mix. My daughter's orders. Enjoy yourself," he said, lifting an eyebrow and shooting a last glance at the two-tone mud-brown suit. A large grin lit up his rosaceous complexion, "You know, Pres, you might want to consider buying a light bulb on the way home."

"You just must meet some very dear, dear friends of mine," she said. "Actually," she lifted her mouth to his ear and spoke in a confidential tone, "they are not all that dear, but they are big supporters of our petition. I think they work for General Motors." With that she set about wedging Waddington into a group of three men who were involved in what appeared to be a very private discussion.

"Do you three gentlemen know Mr. Waddington? No, you probably don't. But now you do. You all work in the automotive industry, different companies, of course, but I'm sure you have a lot in common. Mr. Waddington is the company training manager, and I presume he writes other things too. Isn't that right?" she asked for confirmation.

"Essentially," he said modestly.

Having her presumption confirmed, she turned back to the three men, "Since you're all involved with cars, I'm sure you'll have a great deal to talk about."

Waddington had no idea what Mrs. Fair's normal relationship was to vodka, but it was clear that it was having its way with her, at least on this afternoon. She exhibited a muddled perkiness, surrounded by a frothy gaiety that she did not wear well. The three men from General Motors did their best to appear not to notice. After she'd fluttered off, the men turned to Waddington, their expressions were all the comment needed to express their instant disdain for the writer of training programs in the two-tone, mud-brown suit. Just before they took evasive action and expressed urgent reasons to be some place else, the GM dark-grey suits gave him a collective look that said, please disintegrate.

Waddington again found himself in a group of one, with not even a drink in his hand to make it look like the waiters, at least, were prepared to acknowledge his presence. A waiter with a tray of white wine passed near, and he was able to snag a glass. It wasn't much cover, but it was some. At least he looked like he belonged there. *Ah, the ceiling. I will look like I'm intently studying the ceiling. Maybe people will mistake me for an art aficionado ... or a painter ... or in this suit, I could be a building inspector. Take your pick people. Whatever assumption you make,* he thought, *that's why I'm standing alone looking at the ceiling.*

Like a humming bird revisiting a promising flower, Olivia swooped in on him, once again hovering directly in front of him, staring. "Has anyone ever told you, Mr. Waddington, that you have a very sensitive face? You look like a man who feels ..." she paused sifting words through those brain cells that had not been anesthetized by the vodka until she came up with the right one, "deeply. Yes, I sense a depth."

Like a woman taking charge of a reluctant dance partner, she took his hand and led him to an older, somewhat despondent-looking fellow whose current interest seemed to be that of holding up a wall. When he spoke, his jaw and lips barely moved, giving the impression that he was a ventriloquist without a dummy.

She introduced him as Dr. SomebodyorOther and began to give Waddington a short biography of the man, as if knowing the ventriloquist's accomplishments might help Waddington initiate a conversation. Waddington appeared to be listening intently to Olivia, but, in fact, he barely heard a word. His entire inner being was fixated on her face. He knew he was staring, but could not force himself to look away. So intense was his gaze that at one point, Olivia interrupted herself, gave him an embarrassed smile as if to ask, What? Have I got food on my lip? Has my mascara run? What is it you're staring at? Instead she said, "I'm sorry, I am rattling on. Was there something you wanted to say?"

In fact, there was a lot he wanted to say, none of which would have been appropriate at the moment. Instead he fumbled for an apology, "No, no, I'm sorry if I was staring; I was fascinated by what you were saying." He hoped it didn't sound too lame; especially considering he had no idea what she'd been talking about.

Olivia's smile indicated she accepted his explanation and continued.

Waddington availed himself of the first opportunity to return his attention to her face, this time covering himself by bobbing his head as one fully absorbed. What was it that was so unusual, so compelling about her face? Then it dawned on him. Her face was off-center. All her features, her nose, her mouth, her chin, her eyes were just slightly off-center to the left. It was as if a clay sculptor had created the face and than accidentally bumped it. The slight distortion had left her with a visage that demanded to be looked at, absorbed, appreciated, and studied from different perspectives. He had no idea if anyone else shared his appreciation of that face, but like most art, beauty is in the eye of the beholder, and he suddenly had an urge to behold her, to possess that face, to capture it, to hold it in his hands. He was about to ask her to dance, and would have, but fortunately gathered his wits in time to realize there was no music. He resigned himself to imagining what it would be like to orbit within inches of that face.

Dr. SomebodyorOther turned away to accept another drink from a passing waiter. Olivia glanced first to the left and then to the right, as if checking to confirm that no one could overhear her. She drew up close to Waddington and put her mouth near his ear and whispered, "May I tell you something?"

Waddington nodded.

"I feel like I'm on display. Would you believe it? There are people here I've never seen before who have come just to see what kind of woman Charlie married. I'm sure I must disappoint them." The vodka was now attacking the part of her brain that controlled her ability to enunciate her words.

Before Waddington could argue that she could not possibly be a disappointment to anyone, she said, "You have the face of someone who looks like they'd be easy to talk to."

The butler from Maubeuge appeared and whispered something in her ear. Olivia drained the last of her vodka and excused herself saying, "I must see to our brunch." She nodded toward Dr. SomebodyorOther. "I'm sure you two will have much to talk about."

Waddington noticed that as Olivia walked away, she seemed to alternate first on a leeward tack and then to starboard. *Mrs. Fair is not going to be vertical much longer,* he thought.

III

He watched her until the sea of dark-gray suits and Tiffany ornamentation swallowed her up. This was unlike him. What kind of spell had this woman put on him? It wasn't Waddington's nature to find himself so muddled by the mere physical presence of a woman, particularly one who happened to be the president's wife. Strange, he thought. Strange the effect she'd had on him.

It had to be the excess of testosterone, which he claimed was building up since Muffy had decided sex was a stimulant that made her hungry, and by making her hungry, made her eat, which, in turn, made her fat. So much for exercising his conjugal rights. Yes, that had to be it. He was oversexed and under satisfied. Nevertheless, it certainly wasn't good form to begin fantasizing about the president's wife. He turned to Dr. SomebodyorOther, who was now letting the wall hold him up. Like a horse, his knees were locked and he was nearly asleep on his feet.

Once again, he was alone. This time with a standing, sleeping ventriloquist. His thoughts turned to finding Muffy. He last saw her with a group of women in yet another animated discussion near the French doors that opened onto the terrace. She would not look kindly on having to provide him with social cover. That left him with nothing else to do but wander around the room, looking at the paintings and antiques. It was an incredible home, marble floors, marble columns, marble staircase; an entire marble forest must have been sacrificed to build this house. The period art, the French antiques, the Oriental rugs, it was not just the quality of the items that impressed him, but the abundance.

The living room and what he could see of the terrace leading to the gardens were very crowded now. Obviously, more people had arrived and the frequency with which the waiters came and went with wine and Champagne glasses and special drink orders suggested that they had not had time to attend to the brunch. Maybe there wasn't going to be a brunch. Maybe, at this level of society, the mimosas and Bloody Marys and hors d'oeuvres were considered to be brunch enough. *One thing is for sure,* he thought. *If this group doesn't get some food, and a lot of coffee, they'd better get the kids and old ladies off the streets of Grosse*

Pointe. If there were designated drivers among the guests, they had certainly lost their designation.

Waddington became aware that the decibel level was rising. Conversations seemed to have taken on a lighter note, or so he presumed, because the buzz of voices was now frequently being broken with throaty guffaws and shills of high-pitched peals of laughter. Waddington made his way through the open French doors and found a spot on the terrace that offered tacit invitation to view the magnificent flowerbeds and garden walks.

He noticed Muffy with a group of people on the far side of the terrace. He could not help but admit that she looked very comfortable there, so much a part of that gathering. Her patrician roots were flowering. He edged closer, keeping himself mostly out of sight behind a large cement lion standing guard on the terrace. Waddington counted seven people, Muffy, Olivia, who had alighted there momentarily, plus three other women and two dark-gray suits. They were laughing with the kind of alcohol-liberated hilarity that causes tears to roll down cheeks and breath to come in gasps.

As he watched Muffy orchestrating the conversation, clearly having won acceptance as an equal, he realized just how total the transformation had been from social rebel to social climber. There she was, enjoying the company of people who, like her, were lending their names (she was using her Grandfather's last name), their pocketbooks (ditto), and preparing to give a day out of their important lives (which day had not been decided) to picket the governor's office to express their opposition to the Grosse Pointe low-income housing project.

Muffy's voice rose from the group, moving an octave higher as it did when she was in a snit, though there was no sign of that.

"I told him I had no intention of becoming a breed sow." Muffy announced. "My God, he wanted six kids!"

Three, Waddington corrected silently.

"Can you imagine what six kids would do to your uterus? After Hildy, I told him he had to keep a sock on Mr. Winky." All the women and one or two of the men standing in the conversation laughed convulsively. She was certainly on a roll. And at his expense.

Waddington realized that Olivia had spotted him and was watching for a reaction. He determined he would maintain an indifferent expression, just a guest strolling casually about the terrace. He wandered back toward the house, stepped into the living room, and wondered if anyone would notice if he slipped out of sight behind the drapes.

A call from nature. An excuse to escape, at least for a while. Now where would whoever designed this house have put the bathroom? He asked one of the waitresses to point him toward "the powder room." While a "powder room" sounded a bit effeminate, it seemed more genteel than *john* or *toilet*; certainly *privy* was inappropriate. The waitress directed him toward an arch that led to a long hall. Waddington found the bathroom, as had several other guests who waited patiently exchanging waiting-for-the-bathroom small talk. He returned to the living room and cornered a waiter, "Is there another bathroom, I might use? That one," he gestured toward the hall, "has quite a line. It's a bit of an emergency," he confided in a whisper.

"You might try upstairs. Goddamn, man, this place has got more toilets than a bus station." The waiter's graphic description suggested he was new to the Grosse Pointe catering scene. "Just look around up there and take your pick."

He climbed the stairs and found himself with a hallway on the left and one on the right. He felt like the protagonist in the Lady or the Tiger. He chose the left hall and tried the first door. It opened onto an enormous, formal bedroom, which had to be the master. Probably off-limits to guests. The Fairs certainly wouldn't appreciate his peeing in their bathroom. But there was no one around and his bladder was saying, I'm not going to wait much longer. I intend to explode and what a mess that will be. Off to one side of the room he could see a partially open door. That had to be the bathroom. The oasis beckoned. He'd be in and out in just a minute.

Waddington stepped into the bathroom, turned on the light, and found himself in a bathroom that must have required the sacrifice of another marble forest. He unzipped his fly, lifted the seat on the toilet, and sighed with relief. Oh, nothing like the feeling of relieving a full bladder. And then he heard a voice. "Thank you for lifting the seat."

IV

Waddington reacted as if he's just stuck his finger in a light socket. Immediately he tried to stop the flow. Not easy and very uncomfortable.

"Charlie never raises the seat, and he drips. I hate that. That's why we have separate bathrooms. You're very considerate, Mr. Waddington."

He quickly stuffed his member back into his pants and glanced over his shoulder. Olivia, drink in hand, was leaning again the doorframe. She was smiling at him, but at the same time having a problem keeping her eyes open. She teetered slightly, but appeared to enjoy watching him standing at her toilet. "Please, don't stop on my account. You'll find soap and a towel there on the sink." She started to leave, then turned back to him, "I'll be waiting in my bedroom. I want to talk."

Talk to me? About what? About joining AA? She was very, very drunk. Waddington turned his attention back to the toilet. *Damn! Why didn't I at least lock the door?* His sphincter released and the flow began again. His stream showed no signs of letting up. He was sure he was about to qualify for the *Guinness Book of World Records* for the longest pee. And it was making so much noise. He reached down to flush the toilet to mask the sound from Olivia. When she tells Charlie she found me pissing in their bathroom, I'm history.

Waddington flushed the toilet a second time, put the seat down, and took longer than was necessary washing his hands. He was hoping that if he delayed long enough she'd either leave or pass out on the bed. Judging from her condition, the latter seemed to be a distinct possibly. He replaced the towel, then stepped to the door and peered into the bedroom, praying he'd be able to escape. No chance. She was sitting on the bed, waiting for him.

"Well, Mr. Waddington, isn't it nice to get away from the crowd? I needed a quiet break. Cook is having problems with the Eggs Florentine. I told Charlie we should have fired him. Very noisy … very noisy down there." Her head bobbed. "I do like it quiet. Please," she said, patting the bed, "sit with me for a while."

The last thing Waddington wanted to do was sit on the bed with Mrs. Charlie Fair. There would be no way he could explain the situation to Charlie. He decided to appeal to her hostess role. "Don't you think maybe we should be getting back to your guests?"

"Why? No one will miss me. They're all here to see Charlie. Even the women of my petition committee. They've all come to see my beautiful Charlie." There was resignation in her voice. She looked directly into his face, her eyes searching, evaluating, assessing. "Has anyone ever told you that you have a very kind face, Mr. Waddington?"

Waddington fumbled for a response, but none seemed appropriate. Again, he found himself fascinated with the slightly off-center face. He had the curious impression that she was sending him a tacit invitation, but to what?

"Do you have a first name, Mr. Waddington?" Her eyes locked on his.

"Preston. But, most of my friends call me Pres."

"I would prefer to call you Preston, if you don't mind. It sounds so much more serious than Pres. Are you serious, Preston?"

God, where was this going? Wherever it was headed, he didn't have a road map.

"Please, I would like it so much if you'd sit here," she patted the bed again, "next to me."

Waddington sat down, but a full body width further away from the area she'd patted.

145

"You haven't answered my question, Preston; are you serious?"

"Serious? I'm not sure I understand the question. About my work, you mean?"

"No, about your life ... about ..." She stared off at a large Hudson River School painting that hung over the fireplace. "About the things that really matter ... art ... music ... literature ... the theater. When I was younger, I wanted to be an actress. I was in several plays while I was in college. Are you familiar with *Streetcar Named Desire*?"

"Of course. I loved the movie with Marlon Brando and Vivian Leigh."

"I played the Vivian Leigh part. I was Blanche Dubois. I loved that part. I loved acting."

"Why did you give it up?"

She signed deeply. "For the same reason I've given up so many things in my life: Charlie Fair."

Waddington decided he wasn't going to press for any further explanation.

"Back to my question, are you a serious person?"

Waddington had no choice but to answer, although he was careful to avoid appearing *too* serious. "I suppose I am. At least, somewhat serious. I like classical music. I guess that qualifies me as serious. I used to be serious about acting. I actually spent time in New York trying to be an actor. But, I got serious about trying to make some money to pay the rent and gave it up for a real job."

She looked at him as if he'd just told her he was Russell Crowe. "So, you're an actor?"

Such an adoring look. It thrilled him, but he felt compelled to correct her, "*Was* ... an actor and for hardly more than a couple of months. Now I just read plays for the fun of it."

"Maybe you and I should read together." The idea gave her a sudden burst of sober energy. "We could act out some of the great scenes." She slid off the bed and crossed to the French doors that led to the bedroom balcony and opened them. "We could do Romeo and Juliet, right here. You could climb up the trellis. It's almost like this was made for us."

I don't think so, Waddington thought. *Can't image Charlie Fair having any interest in sponsoring theatricals on his balcony.*

Olivia walked slowly, and not too steadily, back to the bed and sat very close to him, her leg touching his lightly. Waddington felt a ripple of excitement. She had grown serious and her eyes searched his again. Even his optometrist never looked at his eyes this close.

"Forgive me for staring, Preston, but when I look at you I see something I don't see in men very often– sensitivity. You strike me as a man who has the ability to express his deepest emotions. You strike me as a man who would understand how a woman might–" She stopped herself in mid-sentence, as though someone had deleted lines from her script. Then she appeared to pick up a totally different script. "Does your wife always talk about you like that in public?" She didn't wait for an answer. "I thought I was going to like Muffy, but now I'm not so sure."

Waddington didn't exactly spring to Muffy's defense, but he offered an excuse. "I think maybe she's had a little too much to drink. She'd been on a diet and, well, you know."

"I suppose you're aware of what they say about my husband?"

Now where are we going? He began to wonder if Mrs. Fair had a problem staying with one subject. Conversational continuity didn't seem to be one of her strengths. He framed his answer as ambiguously as possible. "They say a lot of things about him. What is it that you've heard people say?"

"They say he's not an easy man to work for."

Waddington would agree with that, but not out loud.

"I would add that the only thing more difficult than working for Charlie Fair is to be one of his sons. He's ruined them, you know?"

He didn't know, but he certainly wasn't going to ask why. This conversation was beginning to put him on edge. Again, he danced away. "How many children do you have?"

"Two. Two boys, twenty-four and twenty-one. They don't live with us anymore. They call me, but refuse to come home." She became melancholy. "He demanded so much of our boys. He would accept nothing less than perfection in their schoolwork, in their sports, in everything, and they just weren't capable of perfection. Look at them today. They're worthless no accounts. Neither has a job. They spend all their time rock climbing and bumming around ski slopes. I don't think either has had a haircut in a year. It hurts me to say it, but they'll never recover from their father. I blame myself for that. I should have been more of a mother and less of a referee. Maybe, if I'd just been stronger with Charlie, I might have …" Her voice trailed off.

Waddington was learning a lot more about the Fair family that he cared to know. Her eyes welled up and a tear found a path down her cheek. He pulled his handkerchief from his breast pocket and offered it to her. Instead of taking the handkerchief, she took his hand and leaned toward him as if she wanted him to wipe the tears away. All he needed now was for someone to walk in and see him sitting on the bed with Olivia, wiping away her tears, and who knew what that someone might think, or worse, say, when he, or she, went back downstairs. He had to find a way to gracefully extract himself.

V

For several moments she sat quietly, her eyes closed, lost in her thoughts. *Maybe she'll fall asleep,* he thought. Waddington waited, hoping she would lie back on the bed so that he could leave before anyone saw him. He was about to ease himself off the bed when her eyes popped open and she turned, looking at him with an intensity that he had not seen before.

"I'm thinking about making a change in my life, Preston. A significant change. My life as it is now just isn't working. Would you like to hear what I have in mind?"

"If you'd like to tell me, that's fine, but …" He decided his best option was to make another attempt at getting her downstairs. "Aren't you concerned that your guests might be wondering where you are? I wouldn't want anyone to get the idea that I've run off with you." He laughed nervously to make sure she understood that he was joking.

Olivia didn't laugh, but looked at him with even greater intensity, "I might like it if you did."

She's coming onto me. Me! Why me, for God's sake? A voice deep inside said, *You have got to get out of here ... now.* He knew it was good advice. Yet, he had to admit, he liked what was happening. This woman, albeit vodka numbed, was attracted to him. *Remember where you are,* the voice warned.

Waddington stood up, actually bolted up, which caught Olivia by surprise. He walked over to the mantle and picked up a large framed wedding photo. It showed Charlie and Olivia in front of a church alter, smiling at the camera. "You made a very pretty bride."

"And an expectant mother," she added. "I was about two months pregnant when we got married."

Waddington put the picture back, gingerly. Here was something else about Olivia and Charlie he didn't need to know.

"Don't' get me wrong, we didn't *have* to get married, we wanted to get married. We just did things in reverse and got pregnant first. If I hadn't gotten pregnant, we might not have gotten married and we wanted to get married. Do you understand?"

Waddington didn't understand at all.

Olivia read his confusion and felt compelled to explain. "You see, my father didn't like Charlie; he didn't trust him, and he didn't want him within a hundred miles of me. He thought Charlie Fair was a fortune hunter, and maybe he was, but that didn't matter to me. I had never had anybody that handsome in love with me. I wanted to kill my father the first time I invited Charlie to come visit. He'd been there for less than twelve hours. He was sleeping in one of the guest rooms and my father woke him up at about five-thirty that morning and said, 'Young man, I don't like you. I don't want you in my house, and I certainly don't want you dating my daughter. I have, in my hand, a ticket for a bus that will be leaving in exactly thirty-five minutes. I expect you to be on it. Get my drift?'"

"What did Charlie do?" Waddington asked.

"He caught Daddy's drift and caught the bus."

"Obviously, he came back."

"Oh, yes, he was very determined. But so was Daddy. He wouldn't let him in the house. So I began to meet him in different places. It became a kind of game. Charlie really seemed to love me in those days, and I loved him. I tried to talk Daddy into giving him a chance, but he felt he was just a pretty boy looking for a meal ticket. Of course, later, he learned that Charlie had a lot to offer, and that he really had a feel for the car business. But that was later. So with Daddy refusing to let us get married, Charlie decided there was only one thing we could do. I had to get pregnant."

"A natural problem-solver, your husband." Waddington's cynicism had just slipped out.

A soulful smile crossed her face. "Yes, I guess he is. Anyway, I got pregnant and when it was confirmed, he went to Daddy and told him he was prepared to do the *right* thing. Daddy gave in. Charlie really didn't give him much choice."

"I'm surprised that your father ever forgave him. I guess he did, though. Otherwise how could Charlie be where he is today?" That really sounded cynical, and he decided to backtrack. "I don't mean to say that Charlie wouldn't have been made president on his own merit, but ..."

151

Olivia jumped in and finished the thought for him, "… but, it helped to have his father-in-law running the company, was what you were about to say."

"Well, I …" Waddington had no idea how to respond.

Apparently, she needed no response. "Actually, I'm not sure that deep down in his heart Daddy has ever really forgiven him. Daddy did not appreciate being boxed in and having no option but to let us gets married."

Waddington decided to become supportive, "Well, it seems to have worked out. You two have been married a long time and there's something to be said for that these days."

"Yes, we have been married a long time," she replied flatly. When she began again, there was resentment in her voice. "But it's no secret that my husband has … well, shall we say he has any number of other interests, which he pursues with far more vigor than our marriage, if you know what I mean?"

Waddington knew very well what she meant, but there was nothing he could say. He wondered how best he might derail the direction of this conversation before it went places he didn't want to go. Again, words failed him.

"I know the question most of my friends would like to ask is whether I am aware of his infidelity." A wan smile crossed her face and she repressed a brief laugh. "If they asked, I'm not sure I would have the courage to answer. I'm not a good liar."

It had to be the vodka talking or whatever else she had been drinking. He could simply not understand why she had selected him, someone she had never laid eyes on, to be her confidant. All the signs said quicksand ahead and he wasn't about to venture any further. He would simply say that he and Muffy had to go home, excuse himself, and leave.

She wasn't about to let him. "I'm afraid, I owe you an apology," she said abruptly.

"What for?"

"For confiding in you the way I have. I know I'm talking gibberish, and I'm embarrassing myself. I'm sure it's the vodka. I really shouldn't have burdened you this way. I have no idea what's brought this on. I guess ..." her eyes seem to plead for his understanding. "I guess I just needed to talk to someone. And when I first saw you downstairs, I said, 'There is a man who will listen.' I don't know what it was, but I felt I could confide in you. And I needed someone to confide in. Please, Preston, sit down beside me again. I find talking to you to be such a comfort."

He hesitated.

"Please," she held up her hand, the one without the Hope Diamond, and let her eyes do the rest. He sat down. She moved very close to him. *Very* close. She pressed her leg against this thigh. "You see, Preston, I'm about to make a significant change in my life." Her tone had become somber, even slightly ominous. "I've decided to do something. My mind is made up and no one is going to convince me otherwise. I'm going to ... I'm going to ..." She paused and looked away, taking a moment to compose herself for the announcement. She picked up where she'd left off. "I'm going to ... go ..." her eyes close slightly as the vodka reasserted itself. "... shopping ..."

Shopping? he asked himself. *She's going shopping? This is the change in her life? What is she talking about?*

And then she told him. "I'm going to go shopping for an affair. I want to take a lover."

He choked back a chuckle. "That should be *some* shopping trip." He really hadn't meant his response to sound as flip as it did. It just came out that way.

"Then you approve?"

"Of your taking a lover?"

"Yes."

How to answer? "I guess you could say ... ahh ... I don't think I'm really in a position to pass judgment on any decision that someone decides to make. I mean, if that person wasn't me making the decision ... then passing judgment isn't my place ... if you know what I mean?" Waddington wasn't sure even he knew what he meant.

Her eyes danced with excitement. She had presumed acceptance. "What you're saying is that you want what I want." She was looking at him intently again; the passion was building like a magnetic force. "And all I want is someone who will truly love me. For me. And not for what my father can do for them or for my money. Just me. You see, Preston, I am just a love sponge."

"A love sponge?" Certainly Webster wasn't going to define that term for him.

"I need love." She was slurring her words badly and fighting to keep her eyelids open. "But it's been so long since there has been any love for me to soak up. I've become very dry ... emotionally, that is." She took his arm and laid her head on his shoulder. "For what

154

it's worth, Charlie and I haven't shared a bedroom or even a bed for years."

In that instant she had assumed the shopping position and Waddington began to feel like merchandise on the shelf.

Me? he asked himself. *She wants to have an affair with me?* It was surreal. Here was this rich, attractive woman shopping for a man at a Wal-Mart when she could have been scooping up good-looking studs at Ralph Lauren. All of them would be more than happy to wet her sponge. Clearly, the vodka had prevailed. And yet, he had to admit he was flattered that she had chosen him, short-lived as that choice was destined to be. Other than Muffy, no woman had even found him remotely attractive or come on to him like this.

Sitting there, feeling her leg pressed against his, her face within a breath, he sensed that all he had to do was raise his hands, take her breasts, and she would respond by bringing her mouth to his. The prospect of holding those marvelous breasts and kissing that mouth made him light-headed. No, he was actually dizzy. For a moment, she opened her eyes and looked up at him. He sensed in that moment that she was waiting for him to take charge, to do something. But what? He was a little short on experience when it came to seduction. Particularly when the seducee is one, totally inebriated, and two, the president's wife. It echoed in his ears, the president's wife. *The president's wife? Are you nuts?* the voice inside him screamed. *Being found with the president's wife, sitting on the president's bed, will put you on a fast-track to losing your job, your wife, and your head.*

155

Her eyes closed again. She could fight it no longer. Her empty glass rolled onto the floor, her head fell back off his arm, and she began to slip off the end of the bed. Waddington caught her before she reached the floor, picked her up, and carried her around to the head of the bed. For a moment, her eyes opened and looked up at him with a satisfied smile.

"Whoever you are, I have always depended on the kindness of strangers." With that she passed out.

Whoever I am? She's so drunk, she's forgotten my name. Maybe that was a good thing. Waddington slowly positioned her on the bed with a pillow under her head. Her last statement before passing out sounded familiar to him. What was it? Then it came to him. Blanche. In *Streetcar Named Desire*. That was her line as they took her off to the loony bin. What a great exit line for Olivia, he thought. Waddington covered her with a blanket and bent close to here face and whispered, "I'm a little bit in love with you, Olivia Fair." He hadn't felt this kind of excitement for a woman in a long, long time. *I should feel guilty about what I'm thinking, but I don't.*

Waddington took one last long look at her fascinating, slightly off-center face. It would probably be the last time he would see her–this close, certainly. In the morning, she would wake and, hopefully, have little, or no, memory of their conversation. He prayed that would be the case. He noticed her lips parted slightly. Waddington found himself confronting an overwhelming desire to kiss that mouth. Oh, what a mouth that would be to kiss. And then he did, lightly.

Waddington walked quickly to the bedroom door, opened it, and peered into the hallway to be sure it was empty. It was. He slipped out, closed the door, then hurried to the staircase and began to amble down, stopping to admire the paintings, just another guest on tour. As he reached the bottom of the stairs, he noticed it was after four and that the brunch had finally appeared. Most of the guests had already foraged through the opulent display of food, leaving it looking like a garden stripped by locusts. He paused and glanced back upstairs, dwelling on the kiss he had given Olivia. He felt like a schoolboy who had copped his first feel from a date who had fallen asleep in a car at a drive-in. He wasn't exactly proud of it, but he'd do it again … anytime.

Herding Cats

Bumper McCoy, who could be counted among the filthy rich of Centerport, was quite fond of his gardener's son, Tom Parker. Tom, as a teenager, worked with his father to mow the McCoy lawn, rake the leaves, weed the gardens, clean the gutters and generally do whatever Bump felt upkeep was needed on his property. Unlike so many of Centerport's young men who never held a summer job, Tom was not afraid of hard work, saved his money for college, was honest, bright, and was always respectful of his elders. Bump admired those qualities, though he was at a lost to understand why, after Tom graduated from college, he was determined to go to work for a TV commercial production company.

` "I know it sounds unrealistic, but I want to be a film director," Tom told Bumper, "and I'm willing to do just about anything if I can get a foot in the door."

Wanting to help the boy, Bumper called on his neighbor Marty Oppenheimer - in the uber rich class - who owned a production company with facilities in New York and Los Angeles, and asked him if he might find a job for the young man. Oppenheimer, who was indebted to Bumper for having bailed him out when his company fell into an economic pothole, was happy to oblige. Oppenheimer told Bumper to send the boy to his New York office and he'd instruct his office manger to find him a job. The favor done, Oppenheimer never gave it or Tom another thought.

Tom arrived at the production office and, as instructed, asked for Vivian, the office manger. After answering several questions about his knowledge of mid-town Manhattan, she said, "Glad you're here, we've been looking for another gopher."

Gopher? Did she say gopher? Tom asked himself. *What does a rodent have to do with this job?* Tom just nodded inconclusively doing his best not to let his face reveal that he had no idea what the tall, reasonably attractive woman with hair piled high on her head was talking about.

"You'll go-fer coffee, go-fer pickups at the film lab, and go-fer pick-ups at the ad agencies. Ok?"

Go-fer! The light came on. *Go-fer this! Go-fer that! This is not exactly the job I'd been hoping for,* he thought, *but...well, everybody has to start somewhere.*

Tom found that many of his go-fer errands involved picking up story boards for commercials and bringing them back to one of the company's several account executives. It was on one such go-fer pick-up that led to his first exposure to the production of a commercial.

"Storyboards from Jordan, Day and Green," he said placing a large envelope on John Baskham's desk.

"The Tasti-Feast commercial?" Baskham asked.

Tom nodded. "And a blueprint for a disaster."

"What makes you say that?"

"I took a look at the boards on the way back from the agency. I don't know who dreamed up this commercial, but they clearly don't know much about cats. Believe me, my sister had six at one time. I know from cats. Anyway, if I'm reading the boards right, the woman puts down a bowl of Tasti-Feast and all of a

159

sudden dozens and dozens of cats appear from every direction making a dash for the food."

"And …?

"Well, unless the director is Dr. Doolittle and can talk to the animals, the cats are not about to line up like it shows in the storyboard and take their turn at the Tasti-Feast bowl. What you're going to have is one hell of a catfight."

Baskham smiled. "Should make for an interesting shoot."

"I gather you're not concerned."

"Nope. Not my problem. I'm just a lowly account executive. This commercial is the personal baby of the ad agency's creative director who, in my humble opinion, ranks as one of the premier assholes of all time. He's going to direct the spot himself because our guys—how did he put it? 'Don't know how to handle pussy.'"

"And he does?"

"The point is, we're not shooting pussy, we're shooting cats. And you're right, it could be a disaster. You wanna come watch?"

"Sure!" Tom said enthusiastically. "But I don't think Vivian will let me out of here."

"Leave that to me. The crew call is for eight Thursday morning at our 54th Street sound stage."

Tom arrived at the studio just as the crew was beginning to light the set - what there was of it. The commercial was to be shot against a totally white background. The stage floor and the walls had been painted white to create a sense of infinity. In the middle of the stage the prop man had hung a window frame.

Below it, he had placed a stove, refrigerator, sink, counter area and two stools, to suggest a kitchen.

The storyboard called for a woman to enter carrying a bowl with the words Tasti-Feast on the side. She was to set the bowl on the counter and, as she filled it with Tasti-Feast say, "We decided to conduct a Tasti-Feast taste test. In this bowl, Tasti-Feast. A wonderful blend of fish and meat." At that point the camera was to reveal five other bowls placed in a neat row on the floor. She was to go on to say, "In these bowls, five competitive brands. Let's see which cat food discerning cats like yours prefer."

She was to set down the Tasti-Feast bowl next to the competitive brands and then, from all sides of the studio, a dozens and dozens of cats were to rush from every direction and make a beeline for the Tasti-Feast. Once the cats had selected the sponsor's brand over the competitors' the actress was to say, "There you have it, proof that discerning cats prefer Tasti-Feast."

At nine, Tom watched the animal handlers arrive on the stage with twenty cages of cats that appeared to be anything but happy about their upcoming participation in the commercial.

"Are those the fuckin' cats?" Tom turned toward the foghorn-like voice, which belonged to Jackson Korman, the man Baskham had pointed out as the creative director from Jordan, Day and Green. He was short, but very wide and walked like a wounded duck. His face seemed to be locked in perpetual sneer.

"All fifty," the animal handler answered.

"They're hungry, right?" Korman looked at the cages as he put the question to the animal handler.

"Really hungry. Haven't fed them a thing since yesterday."

"Good. I want those little fuckers ravenous."

The animal handler turned to Korman. "There's only one thing, being as hungry as they are, there's a good chance they're going to eat everything you set out for them. Including the competitors' food."

"No chance. I've put so much disgusting shit in the brand 'X', 'Y' and 'Z' cat foods that the smell will have them tossing up fur balls before they get within two feet of those bowls."

"But that isn't exactly a fair comparison, is it?" the handler asked.

"Fair? Who's talkin' fair? I'll tell you what's fair. What's fair is that the fucking cats eat the Tasti-Feast and we end up with a great commercial. All you have to do is turn those cats loose when I give you the cue."

At nine-thirty, a large contingent of sycophants and minor functionaries arrived from Jordan, Day and Green, along with Tom Martin, the brand manager from Tasti-Feast. The agency people immediately descended like locusts on the breakfast spread that the catering service had set up in the rear of the studio. It looked to Tom as if none of them had eaten in weeks.

"Hungry group, aren't they?" Baskham said to Tom.

"Almost as hungry as those cats," Tom replied.

"G'morning, John," Tom Martin said as he stuck out his hand to Baskham. "Is this going to work?" he asked, nodding toward the set.

"Korman says it is."

"I didn't ask him, I asked you."

"I'll let you know in a couple of hours."

162

"In a couple of hours, I won't need to ask."

Tom turned his attention to the set where Korman was telling the camera crews where to place the five cameras he'd ordered to cover the action. At least, Tom thought, Korman recognized that he wasn't going to be able to get more than one or two takes of the cats rushing onto the set.

"I don't think they had that many cameras to shoot the chariot race in Ben Hur," Baskham said.

"I've got a feeling he'd better get this on the first take," Tom added.

Korman stood in the middle of the set and shouted. "Listen up, everybody. I'm going to shoot the last scene first. I want to get those cats the hell out of here. Put the cages where I told you," he said to the animal handler, "and have your guys ready to let 'em loose." He then turned to the prop man and said, "Give the bowl of Tasti-Feast to what's-her-face." He pointed toward the actress who was to deliver the lines.

"Maybe I should wear a name tag!" the woman shot back clearly offended that the director had forgotten her name. "It's Angela."

"Angela," he repeated with a shrug. "Ok. Pay attention. On action, you take the cat food, set it down at the end of that line of competitive bowls, and start calling for the cats. Give me a 'Here kitty, kitty.' That will be the cue for the animal guys to open the cages."

The handler and his assistants placed the cat cages around the perimeter of the set, out of camera range. The makeup lady made a quick, last-minute touch-up on Angela's hair, while Korman called for the lights. "Ok, let's get ready to roll film," he shouted.

The actress took her place on the set and Korman turned to the cat handler and his assistants. "You guys ready?"

"Ready."

"Ok, you know your line, right, sweetheart?"

"The name is Angela and I'm not you're sweetheart!"

"We'll talk about that later," Korman's salacious grin made it clear that his retort was for the benefit of his ego and the amusement of the crew. "Stand by and … action!"

The actress looked up at one of the cameras and said, "Let's see which cat food discerning cats like yours prefer." She knelt down on one knee, placed the Tasti-Feast bowl in line with the competitive brands and called, "Here kitty, kitty!"

Korman pointed to the handler. "Cue the cats."

The cage doors opened and the cats dashed out of the cages like convicts during a prison break. Tom watched as a virtual tidal wave of felines surged across the white floor from all directions toward the kitchen set and the bowls of food. As Korman had planned, they avoided the tainted competitors' food and made a rush to the Tasti-Feast.

"Too many cats, too little food," Tom whispered to Baskham.

It was mayhem. A catfight to end all catfights broke out almost at once. Each cat was trying to get to the solitary bowl of Tasti-Feast. The cats treated the kneeling actress as nothing more than a barrier between them and the cat food, a barrier to be pushed, climbed on, slipped under and scratched aside. After failing in an effort to stand up, she toppled back onto her fanny and began to scream. "Get these fucking cats off me! Get them off! Get me out of here!"

"Cut!" Korman yelled.

"Now that would make a hell of a commercial," Tom said, doing his best not to laugh. "Nobody, I mean *nobody*, would forget it."

"Dr. Doolittle he ain't?" Baskham added fully enjoying the mayhem.

The actress screamed obscenities as the cats continued to fight for a chance at the Tasti-Feast.

"I think somebody'd better help her," Tom said volunteering for the job. He hurried onto the white stage floor, made his way through the ravenous cats and literally picked up the actress and carried her out of the melee to the edge of the set.

As he put her down, she spat, "I hate cats! I hate 'em! Look what they did to me!" She showed Tom her scratched arms. "I'm calling my agent!" she screamed at Korman as she stalked off toward the dressing room.

"Get those fuckers back in the cages!" Korman yelled. He ran over to the animal handler, who was attempting to corral a couple of cats and jerked him around, shouting into his face. "What the hell are you doing? Those cats were out of control! This is not what I asked for! Now, get them reset for another take! We got to make some adjustments, cause this ain't going to work." Korman turned his back on the handler and walked off the set calling for a conference with his agency minions.

Martin looked at Baskham, "Unless we figure out some way to save this thing, I'm gonna catch a lot of crap from my boss. I don't know, maybe we should think about calling it a day and going back to the drawing board."

"Your call," Baskham said.

"First, I'm going to have a little chat with our creative genius."

Tom watched as Martin crossed the stage to where Korman was pacing back and forth in front of his staff. Baskham turned to Tom, hardly able to control his amusement. "I can't wait to see how Korman deals with this."

"Set up for take two," Korman shouted. "We're going to try it again. Maybe they won't be as hungry this time."

"Well, there's your answer," Tom said. "It appears he hasn't learned much about cats."

"I think we're going to need a Plan B," Baskham said.

"Can I suggest one?"

"You have an idea?"

"It's something I was thinking about last night. I drew it up, just for the heck of it." He pulled a piece of paper from his shirt pocket and began to unfold it. "It's a lot different from what the storyboard calls for, but I think it makes the same point about the product." He laid the piece of paper in front of Baskham.

"It looks like a maze."

"That's what it is. Sides are about a foot high. And in the center," he said, pointing to a square area in the middle of the maze, "we put the Tasti-Feast. Then we put one cat on the outside of the maze in front of the entrance. We turn the cat loose and let him run through the maze, looking exactly like he knows where he's going until he finds his way to the food. You could shoot it from several different angles, like we're covering a sporting event. You've got five cameras, so each should give the editor a lot of options. Anyway, when the cat gets to the center, the actress says, "Smart cats always find their way to Tasti-Feast."

Baskham said nothing as he digested the concept, then simply, "I love it. One question: Will a cat run the maze?"

"I think so. If he's hungry enough."

"Let's ask the animal handler."

Baskham called the animal handler over and showed him Tom's drawing.

"Yeah, I can get a cat to do that. Do you plan to do it in one shot or a series of cuts?"

"I think it would be more effective if we did it in cuts," Tom said.

"Then it's no problem. Worst case, we'll pull a bag of catnip on a string in front of the cat just out of camera frame."

"Good," Baskham said. "Let's run this by Martin."

"Tom!" Baskham called to the brand manager who was standing off to the side of the set talking to Korman. "Tom, can you come here a minute? I want to show you something."

Martin left Korman, crossed the set and sat down next to Baskham. "This is Tom Parker," Baskham said, nodding toward Tom, who stood behind him, looking over Baskham's shoulder. "He's one of our brighter young guys and he's come up with an idea that I think you ought to look at."

Five minutes later, Martin called for Korman to join them and showed him Tom's concept.

"No, no," Korman said, tossing up his hands to indicate he'd been personally offended that anyone would dare offer an alternative to his creativity. "That's all wrong. Sends the wrong message. I don't like it." Then he looked at Tom and spat out derisively, "Who the hell is this kid to tell me how to make my commercial?"

"*My* commercial," Martin said quietly, but firmly, correcting Korman. "I know this is somewhat of a departure from the storyboard, but I'd really like you to give this some thought. It's simple, it's clean, it's visually interesting and the message is essentially the same as yours."

"Tom, let me be clear about this," Korman said in a condescending, gratuitous tone. "It's a shitty idea. I'm the creative director on this account and I don't like it and that's all there is to it. I'm not going to shoot a cat running in some fucking maze."

"Well, you may be the creative director, but I'm the client," Martin said sternly. "And if you're not going to direct this commercial, then we'll find someone who will."

"You're not serious?" his challenge was tinged with the suspicion that Martin just might be serious.

"Oh, but I am. Further, I think it's best that you and your staff take the rest of the day off. I'll let John Baskham and his people handle this."

"Wait a minute!" Korman said, looking for a retreat. "We need to talk."

"I'm done talking. You might tell Mr. Jordan or Mr. Day or Mr. Green to give me a call when one of them gets a chance."

Korman's face turned red and Tom thought he looked as if he was about to unload on Tom Martin. Tom decided he must have thought better of dumping his vitriol on the client, because he turned away and stalked off the stage, muttering something under his breath.

"Can you find someone to take over, John?" Martin asked.

"John," Tom said, "I can direct this. There's really nothing to direct. We've got five cameras here. We can cover the action five ways to Sunday."

"You know the union says we're supposed to only use Directors Guild members. Do you belong to the DGA?"

"No," Tom said, his face falling

"Who's to know? Get out there and make this thing happen."

II

At just after five, they called it a wrap. Tom Martin walked up to Tom and Baskham, smiling. "For my part, it's been a good day all around. Let me know when I can come see the rough cut."

"Will do," John said.

"Now, I'm going to find myself the nearest bar."

Not ten minutes later, Marty Oppenheimer burst into the studio, spotted Baskham and let loose. The small veins in his cheeks stood out like the blue lines on a road map. "What in the fuck is going on here? I got a call from Jackson Korman. He is pissed as hell." Marty began to jab his finger at Baskham's chest, stopping just short of touching him. "Korman says that we … actually *you*, Baskham … fucked him over with his client. That you went ahead and shot some fucking piece of shit that had nothing to do with his storyboard. I want to know what the fuck happened."

found himself involuntarily taking a step back, but Baskham just folded his arms and listened calmly, touching his face now and then to remove the flying spittle that seemed to punctuate Marty's tirade like exclamation marks.

"Do you want to hear what happened or do you just want to yell at me?"

Oppenheimer shot back, "I want to know what happened."

Baskham proceeded to tell him about the cat melee and how the client was about to cancel the shoot when Tom came up with an idea that Martin loved. "Korman threw a hissy fit and said he wouldn't shoot the new version. So Martin told him to take a hike. The scenic guys built us a maze and we shot Tom's version. Martin loved it."

"Tom? Tom? Who the fuck is Tom?"

Tom stepped forward. "I guess that would be me."

"Are you with the agency or Tasti-Feast?"

"I'm with Ad-Film."

"You work for me?" Oppenheimer had totally forgotten about the favor he had done for Bumper McCoy. "When the hell did we hire you?"

"About a month ago."

"I've never seen you in the office."

"That's because I'm usually out on deliveries or pick-ups."

Oppenheimer turned his back on Tom. With a look of total disbelief, he turned to Baskham, "Is he telling me he's one of our go-fers?"

"Yeah," said Baskham, finding it difficult not to laugh. "That's what he's telling you."

"Jesus H. Christ! Since when did our go-fers start writing commercials? Shit! Did Korman know who the hell he was?"

"All he knew was that Tom had a better idea."

"God damn it! He had no business butting in."

"But Korman's concept was ridiculous. It was never going to work. And Martin told me he would have caught a lot of shit if he'd come back with something that looked like the Revenge of the Vampire Cats. Marty, the truth is, Tom saved the client's ass. I'm sorry if Korman had his delicate creative ego offended. He's a first-class asshole and you know it."

"Get this straight, Baskham. We're in business to provide a production service, not to fuck over some half-assed creative director and to embarrass the shit out of him so that he looks like the dumb fuck that you and I know he is. If the shoot fucks up because the concept stinks and the client decides to call it a day, that's not our problem. They still have to pay us for the shoot."

"Marty, hear what I'm telling you. Tom Martin owes us now. You can bet your sweet bippy that we're going to shoot every one of his Tasti-Feast commercials. His business is locked up for us now."

"Now you hear what I'm telling you," Oppenheimer said, right in Baskham's face. "How many cat food commercials do you think they're going to shoot every year? I'll tell you how many. One! And that one grosses us about fifty grand. On the other hand, Jackson Korman and his ad agency represent about two million dollars of business for us each year. Now you tell me, who's more important to this company? I can't believe you screwed Korman."

"I didn't! It was Martin who made the decision to go with the new commercial."

"Maybe, but you're the one he's pissed at."

"Me? Why isn't Korman pissed at Martin?"

"Because Martin is his client and we are the production company and Jackson Korman can shit on us but he can't shit on his client. Now, listen to me carefully: I want you to get a hold of Korman and apologize like you really fuckin' mean it. I don't care if that means you have to kiss his bare ass in Macy's window. You make goddamn sure we don't lose any of his agency's business. Do you hear what I'm saying? Get it done!"

Marty started to walk toward the door then turned back to Tom. "And what the hell are you doing on the set anyway? I don't pay my go-fers to flake off and watch us shoot commercials." With that, he turned and hurried toward the door.

Then, loud enough so only Baskham could hear, Tom said, "And it was nice meeting you too, Mr. Oppenheimer." He turned to Baskham. "Should I start looking for another job?"

Baskham shook his head. "No. I've known Marty for ten years. By Monday, somebody else will be at the top of his shit list

"What are you going to do? About Korman?"

"I thought I might go over to Macy's and check out their window."

I BLINKED

When I was twelve and about to enter the seventh grade, I remember watching the seniors - grades 7 through 12 were in our same school building - as they strutted through the halls with the kind of haughty superiority that teens display who have finally achieved that pinnacle of their formative years. I could not imagine I would one day be doing the same thing. Then I blinked and found myself accepting my diploma. I blinked again and I was leaving my college campus for the last time. I remember thinking, wasn't it yesterday that I was entering the seventh grade?

In my twenties I was too busy to give any thought to the possibility that one day I would be like any of those old men in my office who seemed to be in a perpetual state of turning fifty. Then I blinked and I was fifty. I blinked again and found myself looking at sixty-five. Now that I've arrived on the wrong side of eighty, I find that I'm doing my best not to blink again as I'm afraid the next time will be the last. Where did all those years go? It was if they were in some sort of competition to see how fast they could erase themselves from my life.

Back when I was in college, I took a literature course that was dominated by the works of Henry James. Two things I remember about James: first he could write a single sentence that would run on and on so long that I would lose track of what was being said and I had to re-read it at least twice, sometimes three times, to get the sense of it. Second, he was the author of a short story that for some reason I fixated on almost to the point of obsession. It's called *The Beast in the Jungle.* The main character is convinced that his life will be defined by some catastrophic or spectacular event and that the event is lying in wait for him like a *beast in the jungle* waiting to spring. I decided to eliminate the idea that I would suffer a catastrophic event. Instead, I became convinced that my life would be defined by a spectacular event and that all I had to do was wait. Well, as I find myself approaching the winter of my years I'm still waiting for *the beast.* Yet, even at my age there is, I believe, time enough left for it to leap into my life.

There might be some who would suggest that my spectacular event had already happened. You see, I came into a great deal of money the old fashion way - the really old-fashioned way. I married it. I'd fallen in love with May Bartram well before I learned she was the scion of old money - old and incredibly abundant money. At the time, I was working for a small advertising agency writing vapid copy for some inconsequential products. She worked for the same company, but in truth she was just playing at working to impress her father. Once we were married she announced, "There's no need for either of us to work. I want us to travel. Daddy has given me his estate here in Centerport and it will be our home, but I want us to travel the world. There's so much to see. If you really feel you need to do something - like work - why don't you become a writer?"

That proved to be easier said than done. Although I let myself labor for years under the delusion that I would one day produce the great American novel, it didn't happen. Not surprising actually, I never got more than a C in English composition.

Even as I grew accustomed and comfortable with my vagabond life of luxury, I continued to believe that the spectacular event - whatever it turned out to be - was lying there in the jungle waiting to leap out. While I waited, May and I took our place among the elite of Centerport, Connecticut, society. May, who at times expressed a tinge of guilt at having acquired her fortune via the luck of her birth, assuaged that guilt by giving lavishly to organizations like the New York Philharmonic, the Metropolitan Opera and various charities and medical research facilities. To her everlasting credit, she never asked for special recognition or a formal thank you. Most of her largess was labeled as having come from that old reliable *anonymous*.

After she died of a tumor at what I consider far too early at 62, I continued to make donations in a haphazard sort of way. I never thought about creating a memorial to her like donating a library to her college or funding a wing at the local hospital. No, the idea of having her name etched in stone over the doorway to some edifice as if it were a substitute for a mausoleum does not appeal to me. I'm sure it would not have appealed to her either. Most people, I believe, do that type of thing not so much because of what it means to the recipient, but what it does for their egos. It's their way of hoping they'll be remembered. But by who? Look at the names on most of the donated buildings in town squares, college campuses and hospitals. Does anyone really know or care who they were? Most names get lost to history in less than a generation.

Let me make it clear that I loved my wife and when she died the idea of finding someone to replace her never entered my mind. Though I was never burdened with being a provider, I was, in nuptial terms, a faithful and attentive husband. I didn't do so well when it came to our children. I'd have to give myself a D on that subject. In truth, both May and I failed as parents leaving them all too often in the care of nannies and shipping them off to boarding schools as soon as they were old enough so as not to encumber our travel lust.

As a result of what I now admit was our neglect, our son has gone through life surfing off Oahu in the summer and playing the ski bum at Aspen in the winter. Our oldest daughter has been divorced twice and, last I heard, was living with a man in Arizona who is a walking tattoo advertisement. The youngest daughter is living *kumbayah* on a commune in California. All of them are sustained by the ample trust funds May insisted on setting up. I think the only reason any of them ever call me is to find out if I'm dead and, if so, to learn what I've left them in my will. I blame myself for their not wanting to have anything to do with me. Maybe, as I think about it now, the beast in the jungle was not a spectacular event, but the catastrophes that my children's lives have become. I hope not.

My days, once I turned eighty, have been without drama and sadly without purpose. Sometimes I have George - he's worked for us since well before May died - drive me from Centerport to the City to attend a concert at the Philharmonic or Carnegie Hall. I used to go to plays, but I don't any more unless they do a revival of a Rodgers and Hammerstein musical or maybe something by Gershwin or Cole Porter. Today's music - if you want to call it that - well, I don't understand how they can call it music. Noise is more like it. I once told some young woman that I loved Mahler. She responded by asking what rock group he was with.

I usually take a few weeks during the summer to have George and our maid drive me up to my farm - though it's not really a farm - in the Adirondacks. I decided to take up fly fishing after I retired. I'm no good at it. But I walk down to the river that runs across the front of my property and picture myself waiting for a fish to rise like the old man at the end of the movie *A River Runs Though It*.

The only thing in my life that might qualify as a routine right now - inconsequential as it is - is my Sunday morning brunch at the Fleur De Lis restaurant in Centerport. May loved to go there for brunch when we were in town. Pierre, the owner - don't think I ever asked him his last name - always puts me at the same table and has a copy of the Times waiting.

It was one Sunday in June that I first laid eyes on Bob Kitzerow and his family. I had only been seated long enough for Heather - she always waits on me - to serve my first cup of coffee when I looked up as a man and woman and three children - who all looked to be under ten - walked in. They were greeted by the hostess - I guess she was new, as I'd never seen her before - who promptly seated them at a table next to mine. While they were dressed in what my mother would

177

have labeled as their "Sunday best," to be honest I immediately regarded the family as an intrusion on what I had come to regard as my private space in the restaurant. *My god*, I thought, *so much for a quiet brunch.*

I waited for the first screaming and childish outbursts that I knew would come while I considered asking Pierre if he would be merciful and move me to another table. But within a few minutes I changed my mind. The three children were perfectly well behaved. No screams, shouts, loud talk or behavioral reprimands from embarrassed parents. No, the family was a Norman Rockwell paining.

Our three children, when they were that age, were always out of control. It got so that a family visit to any restaurant was an ordeal to be strictly avoided. It was only when they were in their teens and home from boarding school that they remained quiet during our few restaurant outings, saying nothing to either their mother or me. Total silence was their way of punishing us for having been forced to dine out with two people whose opinions they considered antediluvian and whose conversation was terminally dull. No, the family next to me that Sunday bore no resemblance to mine - none at all.

The mother appeared to be in her early thirties and, beneath what I must describe as a veil of sadness, she appeared to be very pretty. While she was dressed nicely, she wore little make-up and her hair was pulled back in a casual manner as if she didn't have the time or interest in doing anything more with it. There was something grey about her, almost forlorn even as she looked at her children with the warmth of a woman who took great pride in her issue. The sadness in her expression seemed antithetical to the picture before me.

The father was pleasant looking, an athletic build, brown hair, neatly trimmed. He had the kind of face that looked like people would mistake him for someone they knew, when in fact they did not. He appeared to be making much too much of an effort to remain cheery and buoyant. He talked like one would expect a doting father should talk to small children and it was obvious that they loved him. I could imagine him reading them bedtime stories and then tucking them in at night. It pains me to admit that I seldom did either.

I remember my youngest daughter always asked me to read *Alice in Wonderland* before she went to sleep. I eventually got about half way through and then it seemed I could never find time to finish reading it to her. Eventually, she was able to read it for herself. I wonder if maybe what I have tended to consider one of my inconsequential failures as a parent planted the seeds the eventually led her to find *wonderland* in the arms of the commune.

I could not help but overhear the mother as she looked at the menu. "Can we afford this?" she asked her husband in hushed tones.

"It's your birthday. and the kids and I did not want you to have to make your own birthday lunch."

"We'll skip any appetizers They're too expensive."

"Betty, honey," he said. "It's ok, we can afford this. At least this one time. Please I know you're concerned about the operation. I am too, but I'll find a way to pay for it beyond what our friends and neighbors are doing for us."

"I can't believe all those people want to help."

"You'd do the same for them, if you could. They're good people and one day I'll find a way to pay them back."

I wondered what he was talking about. Operation? What kind of operation? On who? One of the children? Him? Her?

"We'll get through this," the man said laying his hand on her arm. "But let's not talk about that today. This is your birthday and we all want it to be a happy day."

"Daddy ordered you a cake," the youngest one proudly announced.

"You didn't." It was a mild reprimand.

"With candles on it," the child added.

"Hey, Janie, the cake is a surprise. You weren't supposed to tell Mommy," he said gently.

"Daddy are you rich?" the oldest daughter asked

"Oh yes, I'm very rich. I've got three children and a wonderful wife who are worth more than their weight in gold."

"We make you rich?" the daughter asked.

"Oh yes you do. Very, very rich."

At that moment, I found I envied the man. He was indeed rich. More so than I had ever been and I felt compelled to lower my grade as father from a D to an F. Why couldn't I have said something like that to my kids? I was always too busy scolding them. I think I would trade half of everything I own - maybe more - to have been like that man. It was on impulse that I got up and went to the back of the restaurant to find Pierre. The idea had jumped full form in my mind. "Pierre, do me a favor, will you?" I asked.

"Anytime Mr. Marcher," Pierre offered

"Do you know the name of the family at the table next to mine?"

"Their reservation is under the name of Kitzerow."

"Here's what I'd like you to do. I want you to tell them that they are your one thousandth customer and that as a result they have won a free brunch for all five of them. Tell them they can order anything they want and it's all free. Don't worry, I'll pay for it."

"He also ordered a cake."

"It's on me," I said.

"Shall I tell them that you're paying for their brunch?"

"No, please don't. Let them believe this is coming from you."

I went back to my seat and hid behind the *Times* as I listened to Pierre inform the Kitzerows that the brunch would be free. I was able to watch their faces as it appeared the sun had just slipped from behind a cloud and brightened the table.

I listened to their conversation in hope of learning more about the operation, who it was for and who thought so much of them as to raise money to help them pay for it. But nothing more was said. When the cake was delivered, Pierre and Heather led the family in "Happy Birthday," I noticed that tears came to the mother's eyes as she looked first at the cake and then at her children.

"Why is momma crying?" the youngest daughter asked.

"Because she's happy."

I think it was at that moment I mentally adopted them as my surrogate family. I found myself wishing I had the courage to introduce myself and ask to know more about them They looked to be everything my own family should have been, but were not.

George was in the car outside the restaurant and I asked him to wait until we saw the Kitzerow family leave. I had George follow them - at a discreet distance. They left Centerport and drove into neighboring Eastport and made their way to Woodbury Lane. It was an unimposing street with cookie cutter houses - neat, but modest.

George parked the car far enough from their house so as not to draw their attention to my Mercedes which was certainly well out of character for the street. I watched them go inside and was about to tell George to take me home when Kitzerow and his son came out to play catch in their front yard. I tried a couple of times to play catch with my son. But at ten he was uncoordinated, threw like a girl and I made the mistake of telling him so. He got mad, slammed his glove down and went crying to May. From that point on he would have nothing to do with a baseball. I guess I should have tried to give it another go with him, but I never found the time. I watched the father and son for a few minutes. When my guilt got the better of me I told George to take me home.

Maybe it was just out of simple curiosity, or maybe because I wanted to know if they were really the Normal Rockwell painting they appeared to be. The next day I called my lawyer - he's been handing our affairs for years - and said I wanted him to find out all he could about the Kitzerows. What does he do? Which family member needs an operation? Who is raising money to help them pay for it?

He got back to me on Thursday.

"I'm not sure this guy is for real."

"What do you mean?"

"I mean he appears to be a really good man. If his life was a movie they'd bring back Jimmy Stewart to play him. He's a teacher - teaches history and social studies and is also the assistant principal at Eastport High School. Everybody we talked to loves the guy. He's the Lacrosse coach, the town recreation director during the summer, volunteers as an auxiliary fireman, plays the banjo in a four-man band that entertains at a retirement home three times a month, he's on the vestry of his church and volunteers to help out with several charities. And his wife Betty, before she took ill, had a volunteer resume as long as his."

"She's ill?"

"Heart problem. Needs a heart valve operation. But the cost is way over what their insurance will cover so a bunch of townspeople - school kids included, - have been trying to raise money to help pay for it. Trouble is the chances of them ever raising enough before it's too late are pretty remote. I think they know that."

The word remote explained the tears the mother had shed when the birthday cake was delivered and it immediately gave me purpose. The Kitzerows were my family now and their problems were mine. "Find me the best heart surgeon in New York. I don't care about cost. Whatever it is, I'll cover it."

"John, you're talking about a great deal of money. And from what you've told me, you don't really know the Kitzerows. Why do you want to do this?"

"Because I can," I said and added only to myself, *Because I don't want those kids to lose their mother.* "Now please, just make all the arrangements. And if anybody wants to know who's paying the bills, tell them it comes from Mr. Anonymous."

It was two months later that I learned Betty Kitzerow's recuperation from the operation had been a success and that she was doing well. I was also told Bob Kitzerow was making every effort to learn who Mr. Anonymous was. I made sure in that one pursuit he failed.

II

In the years that followed though I never actually met the Kitzerow family, I became a benign stalker. I was like a proud, but invisible, grandparent attending any public event in which Bob or his family participated, but always remaining just another face in the crowd. Whenever I learned that Bob and Betty were helping to raise money for some worthwhile cause, money was donated - anonymously. Charitable goals were met and exceeded. The Kitzerows' fund raising efforts, I learned, had made them kind of celebrities in Eastport. I took a level of satisfaction playing the mysterious Mr. Anonymous that I had not experienced for years.

Sometimes at night, I would drive to Eastport, park on the next block and then stroll through their neighborhood hoping to catch a glimpse of them as if that glimpse would allow me to share a moment of their lives. I quit making my nocturnal visits when a patrol car stopped me one night thinking I might be a peeping Tom. In one regard that's exactly what I was.

Once I attended an Eastport school event in which all three of the Kitzerow children participated. Impulse ruled me again, and I spent the next few days setting up a scholarship fund to cover their costs when it came time for college.

Bob Kitzerow was eventually made principal and word had it that if he decided to run for mayor of Eastport he would be elected unanimously. No one would have wanted to run against him. When a civic group approached him for that purpose he turned them down claiming he could do more for Eastport where it counted by avoiding anything political.

On my ninety-second birthday I got a call from my children. Their trusts were running low and, though they did not say it in so many words, I understood that they wanted to know why I was still coming down for breakfast. Wasn't it time I croaked and replenished their coffers?

Of course it was time, but to irritate them I decided not to die for a few more years. I've since arranged for them to have enough money to live on, but no more than what is needed to keep a roof over their heads and food on the table. I did that mostly out of guilt and for May. The bulk of my money I put into a charitable foundation named for her. My children will be apoplectic when they learn they've been cut out of my will, but c'est la vie.

On the subject of dying: The other day I was watching the History Channel and they were doing a piece on the life and career of the old time actor W.C. Fields. Apparently, just before he died a friend visited him in the hospital and was surprised to find him thumbing through a Bible. Asked what he was doing, Fields replied, "I'm looking for loopholes." I decided to pull down May 's copy of the Bible and after I'd spent some time thumbing through it, I came to the conclusion there were no loopholes left.

The last time I saw the Kitzerows was almost fourteen years to the day when I had seen them first and by chance it was at the Fleur de Lis restaurant. I had just finished my last cup of coffee and was about to leave when they came in and, as fate would have it, they sat at the same table as before. Bob, his wife, their three children - now in their early twenties - and a young woman who appeared to be the son's fiancé, were in a happy animated conversation about the graduation of the middle daughter from Yale. Their voices bubbled with cheerful expectation of the plans they had made for the summer. Bob, I noticed, said little, content just to listen and play the proud father and husband. They had ordered wine and once the glasses were filled he proposed a toast.

"To your mother, my wonderful wife. Happy Birthday Betty. And to whoever it was who made such a difference in our lives."

"To Mr. Anonymous," the middle daughter said and they all laughed.

"Yes, to wonderful Mr. Anonymous," Betty echoed.

What I wouldn't have given for May to have experienced that moment with the Kitzerows. As I got up to leave I noticed Betty gave me a quizzical look and, for a moment, I thought she might have recognized me as the family stalker. I was wrong, she was looking at an old man who was searching for his cane and appeared in need of help navigating to the door. I smiled a smile that said thanks, I could manage and she smiled back and turned her attention to one of the children who'd made a remark that made them all laugh. The delight in their voices followed me like a fresh breeze and I felt that I would carry it with me all the way home.

III

It was on an August evening almost two months later that John Marcher did something he had not done in years. He asked his butler George to help him out to the back terrace so that he could sit in the big, high back Adirondack chair placed so that it maximized his view of his lawn and gardens. The evening air was soft, almost as if the temperature had been dialed to perfect. His eyes followed his great green lawn, past the bordering gardens all the way to the beautiful hand carved figural marble gazebo May had brought back from Italy. *She loved the thing*, he thought. *Said it was like a crown for her gardens.* The sun was sliding lower in the sky sending shadows from the trees creeping across the small ponds that sang their watery song as the fountains sparkled in the sun light. The cumulus clouds that drifted like wads of cotton against the azure sky were turned into a pallet of color as the sun painted them in many various shades of gold, silver, red and purple. "God this is beautiful," he said aloud, surprised by the sound of his own voice.

He thought he heard the terrace door open and turned to watch his wife step out on the terrace carrying a tray with two glasses of Chablis, a small block of cheddar and her favorite crackers. *Remarkable*, he thought, *the years have been so good to her.* "May, look at our yard," he said with a sweeping gesture. It's beautiful, absolutely beautiful. Why haven't we come out here more often just to sit and enjoy this?" He turned back toward his wife, expecting her to answer. But she was not there. "We should have," he said softly as he turned back to the summer tableaus playing out in front of him. "We should have." His head fell back on the chair's headrest. "Beautiful, just beautiful."

Then, as dusk fell like a soft fog, he blinked. And as he blinked he accepted in his last moment that the beast he had expected to leap and define his life could never have happened as he imagined it would. He understood, finally, that it was he who had been the beast in the jungle and the spectacular defining event began the day he sprang - anonymously - into the lives of the Kitzerows.